J. T. EDSON'S
FLOATING OUTFIT

The toughest bunch of Rebels that ever lost a war, they fought for the South, and then for Texas, as the legendary Floating Outfit of "Ole Devil" Hardin's O.D. Connected Ranch.

MARK COUNTER was the best-dressed man in the West: always dressed fit-to-kill. BELLE BOYD was as deadly as she was beautiful, with a "Manhattan" model Colt tucked under her long skirts. THE YSABEL KID was Comanche fast and Texas tough. And the most famous of them all was DUSTY FOG, the ex-cavalryman known as the Rio Hondo Gun Wizard.

J. T. Edson has captured all the excitement and adventure of the raw frontier in this magnificent Western series. Turn the page for a complete list of Berkley Floating Outfit titles.

J. T. EDSON'S
FLOATING OUTFIT
WESTERN ADVENTURES
FROM BERKLEY

J.T. Edson

THE HALF BREED

BERKLEY BOOKS, NEW YORK

Originally published in Great Britain by Brown Watson Limited

This Berkley book contains the complete
text of the original edition.
It has been completely reset in a type face
designed for easy reading, and was printed
from new film.

THE HALF-BREED

A Berkley Book / published by arrangement with
Transworld Publishers, Ltd.

PRINTING HISTORY
Corgi edition published 1969
Berkley edition / February 1981

ISBN: 0-425-04736-9

A BERKLEY BOOK ® TM 757,375
Berkley Books are published by Berkley Publishing Corporation,
200 Madison Avenue, New York, New York 10016.
PRINTED IN THE UNITED STATES OF AMERICA

PART I

The Half-Breed

THE DUN HORSE was running well, its long forelegs reaching out and dragging ground under it, the hind legs propelling the horse forward. Behind him the posse had stopped firing, probably because Sheriff Dickson had told them to stop, but more likely because they saw the futility of trying to hit a fast-riding man from the heaving saddle of a racing horse.

Mort Lewis bent low along the neck of his horse, urging it on yet trying to hold back some reserve in case it was needed. The dun ate work, loved to run and would willingly run until it dropped; the posse were only just holding their own against him. One thing and only one thing was in Mort Lewis's favor: he knew the country better than the pursuing men, knew it as only a man with Indian blood in his veins could know it. Mort Lewis was half Indian. His father had been a man with ideals, one being that he could scratch a living from one horse spread in the hills, the other that one day people would forget he had married a Comanche girl and accept both him and his son into their society. He died without seeing either of his dreams take shape. Mort Lewis was a half-breed; it was made plain to him every time he came to the town of Holbrock. The cowhands accepted him but the other folks, people of the town, kept clear of him. Brenton Humboldt, justice of the peace and businessman, leading citizen of the town, sent his daughter to an Eastern relative because she was friendly with Mort. He then ordered him from the

Humboldt property, swearing that no half breed would ever set foot in his house or on his land.

But there was no danger of that happening now with a posse behind Mort, a posse with three of Dave Stewart's men riding in it. His only hope was to get into the thick wood over the next hill where he might hide until there was a chance to slip through and head for the Comanche country. No posse would dare to follow him into the land of those savage fighting warriors and he would be safe. Even Stewart's three hardcases, Scanlan, Milton and Salar, would not dare to cross the river beyond Sanchez Riley's place for that was the Comanche country, and Chief Long Walker had taken a lodge oath that no white man should enter his land.

The racing dun swung up the slope, sticking to the well-worn surface of the stagecoach trail rather than breaking over the open land where a wrongly placed foot might find a gopher hole. If the dun went down Mort would be at the mercy of the posse which was clinging to his trail like a pack of ravaging wolves. They topped the rim behind him and he heard another couple of shots, but the bullets came nowhere near him. Salar, the best rifleman of them all, was not using his Buffalo Sharps rifle yet; he would save the costly bullets until they ran the dun to a halt. Then from a range Mort's old Spencer carbine could not reach, the Mexican would get down, take careful aim and do what his boss, Dave Stewart, wanted.

Mort's dun rocketed over the top of the rim and down the other side. Once around the blind corner at the bottom he would have a clear run to the woods and a chance of safety. The posse was almost a mile behind him and, crowding on the trail, were slowing each other down.

The young rider was tall, well built, with a reserve of strength in his powerful frame. His hair was black and straight, telling, as did his rather high cheekbones and his coal black eyes, of his Comanche blood. The face

was handsome by European standards and the cheekbones were not too obvious, but they gave sign to men
who knew the West. His clothes were not those of a
working cowhand; he wore a buckskin shirt tucked into
Levis and on his feet were Comanche moccasins. Around
his waist was a gunbelt, a plain-handled Army Colt,
butt forward at his right side. Mort made no attempt to
draw either the revolver or the Spencer carbine, which
showed from the saddleboot under his left leg.

There was no need for him to try and draw the
weapons; he was out of range for both Colt and the
Spencer and he didn't want to kill, not even the men
following him. There were a couple of men in the posse
who'd treated him decently. Sheriff Dickson had given
Mort work as a deputy when one who could read signs
was needed. The rest of the posse were men Mort
wouldn't have spat on if they were on fire, loafers from
the town, men who were willing to jump into any
trouble but would neither work nor wash. To them he
was the half breed and they hated him. Much of the hate
was caused by envy, for Mort could excel them in so
many things. Stewart's men were along to make sure
Mort was not taken alive. That was what Dave Stewart
wanted and what Dave Stewart wanted he usually got.

The blind curve was ahead and Mort hurled the horse
around it. Then he saw the two riders ahead of him.
They had come out of the woods and were blocking his
way. The dun tried to turn, but was traveling too fast. It
lost footing and Mort felt it going down. He tried to
throw his balance to bring the horse back to its feet but
was too late. The dun went down and Mort tried to kick
his feet free of the stirrups and leave the saddle. He was
just too late. The falling horse caught his foot and he
crashed forward. He lit down rolling to break his fall,
the instinct of self-preservation acting through his
winded, dazed body. His Army Colt had been thrown
from his holster and he dived for it as the dun struggled
back to his feet.

The two riders looked young but they reacted with a speed which showed that defending their lives was not an unusual thing for them. The small man on the big paint horse flipped his left hand across his body, the white-handled Colt leaving the holster at his right side in a flickering, sight-defying blur of movement. At the same moment, the tall, dark youngster afork the huge white stallion bent forward and slid the Winchester rifle from his saddleboot, levering a bullet into the breech as he brought it up.

The rifle spat and for a fast-taken shot it was either very lucky or very accurate. The bullet kicked the gun from under Mort's hand; a second shot following to prove that skill, not luck, was behind the hit. The gun was knocked to one side and, as it landed, the second bullet knocked it further away.

"Hold it there, mister!" snapped the smaller man, bringing his horse forward to stand over Mort and lining his Colt down. "Lon could just as easily have downed you as hit the gun."

Mort looked up at the two men. The paint's rider was small, not more than five-foot five or six at most, but he held the gun with the air of a master. He was a handsome, pleasant-looking young man wearing plain range clothes though his low-crowned, black J. B. Stetson hat was expensive and his high-heeled boots were made to measure. His saddle was a well-made, expensive rig, and the big horse showed breeding in every line. The young man did not look the sort to own such a hat, boots, saddle or horse. He looked even less likely to be wearing a buscadero gunbelt with two holsters, and a second white-handled Army Colt, butt forward, at his left side, mate to the revolver held in his left hand.

All in all, that dusty blond-haired youngster might look young and insignificant, but Mort was not fooled. There was that indefinable something which told one cowhand that another was a tophand. This small, grey-eyed youngster on the big paint was all of that: a tophand and one who could handle those matched guns or the Winchester carbine booted at the left of his saddle with more than ordinary skill. He was not the sort of man one could take chances with and his voice showed he expected Mort to obey.

The other man, if man could be the term for he didn't look much more than sixteen years old, was tall and slim. There was a whipcord strength about the youngster, a wiry power which did not seem right for one so young looking. His face was tanned as dark as Mort's own; a strangely young-looking face, innocent in feature, babyish almost, but with red-hazel eyes that were neither young nor innocent. They were cold, hard and menacing as they squinted along the blued barrel of the old yellow boy, lining the V notch of the backsight and the tip of the foresight on Mort's body.

The youngster wore all black, from his hat, his bandanna, shirt and Levis, right down to his boots. Even the gunbelt was black leather and only the walnut grips of the old Dragoon Colt, butt forward at his right side, and the ivory hilt of the bowie knife at his left hand relieved it. He looked wild, alien and almost Indian as he sat the saddle of his seventeen hand white stallion. The horse was a beauty, even bigger and better than the huge paint that the other man rode, and, like the paint, was a horse that no beginner could manage. Both would take a good man to handle them.

Mort saw all this in one swift glance. He heard the posse drawing nearer and flung himself forward. His horse was on its feet but he did not try for the saddle. Instead, he flung himself toward the side of the trail. If he could beat the rifle and the Colt and get into the bushes, he might still get away.

The small cowhand acted fast. He did not shoot but his right hand brought the length of hard-plaited, three-strand Manila rope from the saddlehorn and sent the noose flipping out. Mort heard the hiss of the rope but left it too late; even as he tried to avoid the loop, it fell over his head. The small man pulled back, tightening the loop and pinning Mort's arms to his sides, then quickly dropped two more loops around Mort's shoulders.

"Give it up, friend," the small man drawled, his voice calm, firm and without any sign of animosity. "You can't get away now."

Mort stood still, his face as inscrutable as he could manage. The posse would be in sight any minute now and he knew that he was going to die. If so, he would try and die without disgracing his Comanche mother's blood.

The posse came tearing around the corner, bringing their horses to a sliding halt, hands reaching for weapons as they saw Mort standing in the center of the trail. Leading the men were Stewart's three riders: Scanlan, big, burly and heavy, his bristle-covered, scarred face split in an evil grin as he saw Mort. Milton, lean, cadaverous and a fast man with a gun, sat at the right of the trail. Salar was at the left, a tall, swarthily handsome Mexican who dressed in the height of *charro* fashion: a fancy, silver-decorated bolero jacket, frilly bosomed white silk shirt, trousers which were tight at the waist and thigh but flared out at the bottoms and high-heeled boots with big roweled Spanish spurs. Yet, unlike most Mexicans, he showed no sign of a knife and gave no indication of the Mexican's affinity for steel as a fighting weapon. He was fast with the silver-mounted, nickel-plated Army Colt in the low-hanging holster and a deadly shot with his Sharps Buffalo rifle.

The three men were the pick of Dave Stewart's hard-case crew. They were supposed to be cowhands but their duties were more concerned with enforcing Dave Stewart's will. Scanlan was Stewart's foreman, a hard-fisted, bullying killer. The other two were his companions, and it was rare that one was seen without the other two.

Mort could see no sign of the posse's leader, Sheriff Jerome Dickson, and knew that he would most likely be dead before the sheriff arrived. He felt the rope go slack and the horse move back slightly from him.

"Stopped him for us, did you," grunted Scanlan, glancing at the two cowhands. "Good, the boss'll likely give you a reward." He reached for the rope on his saddle and unstrapped it. "You should have killed him, but we'll soon tend to that."

"Just what do you reckon you're going to do?" asked the small Texan, his voice suddenly hard.

"Going to decorate that cottonwood up there, sonny," replied Scanlan and grinned at the laugh which came from the posse. "See how the breed looks hanging around it."

The small man shook his head, swung from his horse and walked to Mort. The gun was back in leather, Mort saw, and wondered what the youngster hoped to do against the full strength of the posse.

"Oh no!" drawled the small Texan.

Scanlan swung back to face him. Then his eyes went to the Indian-dark, innocent-looking boy. He was lounging in the saddle of his big white with the Winchester rifle resting on his shoulder, his right hand gripping the small of the butt, three fingers folded through the lever of the rifle and the other resting on the trigger. Slowly Scanlan studied the boy, then dropped his eyes to the small man.

"You reckon you can stop us?" he asked, throwing a grin at the other posse members.

"Do *you* reckon I can't?"

Scanlan did not answer for a moment. His eyes went first to the paint horse and then to the white-handled guns which were butt forward in the small cowhand's holsters. A hard grin came to his lips and he nodded understandingly.

"Two guns, slung for a crossdraw, fancy, white-handled guns at that, paint hoss and all," he sneered, mockingly, pleased that he'd got an audience. "Who do you think you are–Dusty Fog."

"Mister," the dark boy spoke for the first time, his voice hard and sardonic under the easy drawl. "He doesn't think. He *knows* he's Dusty Fog."

"Yeah," scoffed Scanlan, throwing a glance at the other men in the posse. "I reckon you'll be the Ysabel Kid, then."

"How'd you all guess?" the dark boy's voice was mocking. "Or did ole Salar there tip you the wink?"

Salar frowned, his eyes narrowed as he looked harder at the young man. Scanlan clearly was not satisfied and his voice dripped sarcasm as he turned his eyes to the small man once more.

"All right, Dusty," he said, waving his hand toward Milton, "This here's Wes Hardin and I'm Wild Bill—"

It was at that moment that the big paint moved so the men could see the brand it carried. Burned on the hip were two letters, an O and a D, the straight edge of the D touched by the side of the O. Scanlan could read the brand, OD Connected, the brand of Ole Devil Hardin's Rio Hondo ranch. Dusty Fog was Ole Devil's nephew.

There was a moment of uncertainty for Scanlan, then he shrugged it off. That short runt could not be Dusty Fog, although the other might be the Ysabel Kid.

"Tell you, Dusty," he went on, forgetting to complete his sarcastic introduction of the other posse members, calling each one the name of a famous gunfighter. "You want for us to ask real nice afore you let's us hang him."

"Mister," the small man's voice was still even. "I'd show you my card, but I doubt if you can read. One thing I do know. The only way you can hang this feller is by passing me."

Scanlan lifted his right foot to step forward, then set it down again. His eyes were on the small man, noting the relaxed, casual way he stood; there was no fancy position taking, no sinking into the so-called gunman's crouch. The young man stood erect, hands by his side, yet there was something latent and deadly about him which warned Scanlan more than any amount of words. Suddenly the small man was no longer small, but stood taller than any man there, or so it seemed to Scanlan.

"Shem!" Salar reached his decision and spoke a warning. "That's the Ysabel Kid. I recognize him now."

"Now ain't he the smart one," the dark boy's drawl was mocking. "I recognized him right off at that."

There Scanlan had it laid out before him. The dark boy was the Ysabel Kid and the other one really was Dusty Fog. The thought brought Scanlan to a halt; to hang Mort Lewis, he'd have to pass the guns of Dusty Fog. Scanlan and every man in the posse knew Dusty Fog and something about him.

He was a legend in his own life, the small Texas cowhand called Dusty Fog. In the War he'd been known as one of the South's best cavalry officers. He'd been a captain at seventeen and his name was said in the same breath as John Singleton Mosby and Turner Ashby. They were names which stood at the height of the South's fast-riding, raiding light cavalry. Since the War, Dusty's name was known as a tophand with cattle, a rough mount rider, ranch segundo, trail boss and town-taming lawman. His name ranked high in each of those trades, and among the highest of the fast draw breed. They said he was the fastest gun in Texas.

This was Dusty Fog, the man Scanlan would have dismissed as a nobody, the man Scanlan was forced to face if he meant to hang Mort Lewis.

The other one, that baby-faced, mocking-voiced boy on the big white stallion, he too was a living legend, the Ysabel Kid, Loncey Dalton Ysabel. Down on the Rio Grande stories were told of him from the days when he and his father ran contraband across the river. He was known as a man who could throw lead with some speed and accuracy, disproving the theory that his old four-pound, two-ounce Colt Dragoon gun was long out of date and over-heavy. He was also known to be a fine exponent on the art of cut and slash in the traditional style of the old Texas master, Colonel James Bowie. But it was with his rifle that he was best known, with an old Kentucky rifle, then with the Winchester Model of 66, the old yellow boy. What Dusty Fog was to the handling of revolvers, the Ysabel Kid was to a rifle. There were other things about this dark, dangerous young man. It was said he could speak fluent Spanish and make himself thoroughly understood in six Indian dialects; that he could ride anything with hair and that he could follow a track where a buck Apache would not know how to begin trying.

That was the Ysabel Kid, friend, companion and sidekick of Dusty Fog. He did not need Dusty's aid to bolster his own reputation.

Of all the men in the West, Dusty Fog and the Ysabel Kid were the worst possible for Scanlan's purpose. The two Texans said Mort would not hang and they meant every word they said. Neither would back down and there was only one way to take their prisoner. If Dusty Fog said Mort was not going to hang he would back the words. He was bad enough on his own, but backed by the Ysabel Kid, he was more than a match for Scanlan's two friends and the rest of the posse.

Dusty watched the crowd. Rope-fever was plain on the faces of most of the men. He could read their type as well as he could read their insane desire to see a man kicking at the end of a rope. The loafers wanted to kill, to hang this man so they could boast they'd helped in doing it. There was no desire for justice, nor just cause to wish for hanging, just rope-fever. It was a sickening sight.

Sheriff Dickson came around the corner, trying to urge a better speed from his horse. He saw everything as he came into sight of the men: Mort Lewis standing with a rope around his arms, Scanlan holding his own rope, and the other men behind him. Then Dickson saw the small Texan and the youngster on the white horse, but hardly gave them a second glance. They'd not been in the posse when it left town and must have come on to Mort as he turned the corner. They were lucky Mort Lewis was not a killer, Dickson thought, or they'd have not taken him so easily.

"What's the idea, Scanlan?" Dickson asked.

"We caught Lewis."

"I can see that. What's the rope for?"

Scanlan did not reply. He knew that the sheriff was a man he did not scare. He also knew that Jerome Dickson had warned them that there would be no lynching. One of the saloon hardcases of the posse, not knowing Dickson so well, called out:

"We're going to save the county the money for a trial."

Dickson swung down from the horse. He swore he'd see the livery barn owner about giving him this wind-broken animal to ride in a posse. His own horse was tired and he'd done as usual, sending to the livery barn for another. The horse had looked all right but showed itself unable to keep up with the rest of the posse's mounts. He could guess why. They wanted to get to Mort Lewis before he arrived. If they'd done so Mort would be dead. Dickson was surprised that he was not dead. He felt the eyes of the small cowhand on him and gave Dusty more attention.

Dusty looked at the sheriff. Dickson was a tall, spare man of middle age, his face tanned and strong looking. His brownish moustache was neatly clipped and his clothes were just good enough to show that he was the honest sheriff of a poor county. The gunbelt, with the plain-handled Army Colt showed signs of care and the holster hung just right. Dickson was poor, honest and a good man with a gun. There was a grim look on his face as he turned to the watching posse.

"There'll be no lynching while I'm sheriff," he said.

Scanlan's sneer grew thicker. "Which same won't be long, way you're acting."

"Maybe, but while I am, what I say goes."

"What's he wanted for, sheriff?" Dusty asked.

Dickson was satisfied he was correct: here was a man to be reckoned with. There was the way he stood, the way he looked right at a man, the way his matched guns lay in the holsters of that belt. A man who was among the magic-handed group known as the top guns. Things would go badly if he was to side with the others in wanting to hang Mort Lewis.

"They say he killed a man," Dickson replied, wondering how he had ever thought the other man was small.

"Did he?"

"I don't know. When I went to question him he dived through the window of the Long Glass saloon, back in Holbrock, went afork his horse and lit out of town."

The Ysabel Kid's eyes went to the posse, his contempt plain as he studied the faces of the men.

"Maybe he thought he wouldn't get a chance to tell his story," the Kid said. "That *hombre* there," his left thumb indicated Scanlan, "sounded tolerable eager to have him hung."

"He killed old Dexter Chass, that's why," Scanlan spat out. "Shot poor ole Dexter down without a chance."

"We don't know Mort here did it," Dickson snapped. "I only wanted to ask him where he'd been—"

"Why the hell did he run if he didn't kill old Dexter?" Scanlan growled.

"Lon could have called it right," Dusty replied, never taking his eyes from Scanlan's face. "The feller might have known that he'd never get a chance to say anything, way you're acting."

"That's been said too often," growled Scanlan.

"Mister, happen you don't like it I'll say it again," the Ysabel Kid growled, sounding mean as a starving cougar. "Any time you reckon you can stop me just say the word and let her go."

Scanlan gave this some thought for a few seconds. He'd built up a reputation around Holbrock as being bad medicine and a fast man with a gun, but he made no move to take up the challenge. He tried to tell himself that he refused because the Kid's rifle was out, resting on his right shoulder, but he knew it was a lie. A fast man with a gun stood a good chance of being able to drop his hand and lift up his Colt before the Kid could swing the rifle down and into line. Scanlan knew that, knew it and did not mean to gamble his luck on it, not even when backed by two other good men. There was a reason. The Ysabel Kid was also backed, if only by one man. That man was Dusty Fog and he could copper any bets made by Salar and Milton, then call "keno" at the finish.

Sheriff Dickson could hardly believe his ears. The two young men were willing to side with him against the lynch-minded crowd. There were two more men in the posse who would not take part in any lynching and would side him. That made five against nine. Good odds. Odds that the men who made up the nine would not face down.

"We'll take you back and hold a hearing," Dickson said, taking the chance he was right about the two cowhands. "Will you two gents be riding into town with us?"

"We're headed for Holbrock," agreed Dusty. "We'll ride with you. This is Ysabel Kid, I'm Dusty Fog."

For a moment Dickson suspected a joke but there was no hint of amusement on the faces of the two young men. They were who they claimed to be. That was why Mort Lewis was still alive. Dickson smiled. He'd always suspected Scanlan of being a big-mouthed showoff who would dog it if faced by a good man. Now there was proof and confirmation of the suspicion.

"Be pleased to have you along, Cap'n Fog," he said and he meant it.

Dusty went to look at the dun horse. It was unhurt by the fall and would be able to carry the man back to the town, not more than four or five miles away. Turning he walked back to Mort and removed the rope.

"You're coming back, friend," he said. "I'll give you my word that you'll get a fair hearing. If you try and run, the Kid'll cut down your horse. If you didn't kill the man you'll have nothing to fear."

"Won't I?" Mort answered. "I'm a half breed, Cap'n—."

"So?" Dusty drawled. "I thought the question was whether you killed a man, not who your mammy and pappy were."

"I'll go with you, Cap'n," said Mort, knowing that Dusty did not care whether he was a half-breed or not and would see fair play. "I won't try to run for it again."

Dickson nodded in approval: Mort Lewis was a man of his word. If he said he would ride in then he would do just that and there would be no more attempt at flight. The sheriff bent, picked up Mort's revolver and turned it over in his hands. The loading lever under the barrel was badly buckled and the walnut grips broken but the gun was still in working condition. There'd been some close-called shooting on the weapon, Dickson saw, and thanked his stars that it was Dusty Fog and the Ysabel Kid who had met up with Mort. There were many men who would have shot to kill in the circumstances, not waiting to see what was wrong. Almost any of the posse would have done so, cutting Mort down just to boast they'd done it. His eyes went to the sullen-faced posse as he thrust the revolver into his waistband. The men looked uncomfortable at the scorn in the sheriff's eyes.

"Mount up, all of you," Dickson said.

The Kid, his rifle still resting on his shoulder, eyed the posse with cold distaste. His voice was cutting and menacing as he addressed them:

"You bunch ride a piece in front of us," he ordered. "I don't want you to think I don't trust you – but I don't."

Scanlan's scowl deepened, but he found himself lacking the courage to go against the Kid. His idea had been to get alongside Mort's horse; a quick kick in the dun's side would cause it to leap forward, then Mort could be shot down. A volley would bring him down, there would be no proof that any one man fired the fatal shot and less about how Mort came to try and escape. The Kid's order would cancel any chance of doing the kicking or shooting.

Once more Scanlan thought of trying to call the Kid's hand. If he could make the first move, others of the bunch at his back would join in. Nine to five – Scanlan knew two of the men would not back him – was good odds. The sheriff and the others could be cut down by sheer force of numbers. There was only one thing wrong: Scanlan knew he would not be alive to see it. He would be the first target for the Ysabel Kid and for Dusty Fog.

His eyes met the Kid's, reading the mocking challenge and the supreme confidence in them. More than ever he knew the Kid would welcome any attempt to start something and was ready, willing, and more able to finish whatever was started.

The rest of the posse watched Scanlan, knowing everything hinged on him. The men who did not work for Stewart were thinking things over; Salar and Milton just waited for their friend to call the play. Scanlan knew it, knew the others expected him to do something. It hurt to know he dare not make a move. With an angry growl he turned and mounted his horse, wrenching cruelly at its jaw as he rode through the other men.

It was a silent and sullen posse which headed toward
the town. There was no talking by anyone, the men in
the posse watching Scanlan, the leader who had failed to
come through, and wondering what had made them
think he was tough. The sheriff was watching Mort
Lewis and the two Texans. There was relief on
Dickson's face as he glanced at the small Texan; with
Dusty Fog at his back he could conduct a proper inquiry
into the killing of old Dexter Chass. There was not
much to go on so far. The only hard fact against Mort
was his running away, and even that could be explained
as Dusty had already explained it. There was much cir-
cumstantial evidence against Mort, but it could be
blasted easily enough.

The town of Holbrock was small, sleepy looking and
peaceful. It was the sort of town which existed in the
hundreds through the cattle country of Texas, a small
place which never received the publicity of Fort Worth,
Dallas or other cowland hot spots. It was doubtful if
Holbrock was known beyond the county line; nothing
much ever happened there and the town went along its
peaceful way.

The scattering of houses backed off the main street,
an untidy straggling double line of stores, a couple
of saloons, a dance and gambling hall and the county
offices, a large building and the most expensive building
in the town, containing the county office, sheriff's
office, jail and town marshal's office. The latter was
never used as the town found they could not afford to
hire a full-time marshal after paying for the splendid
building. The leading citizen, Brenton Humboldt,
boasted that his project, a vaguely defined idea, would
bring money pouring into Holbrock, making the town
boom; this building would then be of great use to the
county seat.

The return of the posse attracted interest and there
was a rapid gathering of men at the Long Glass saloon,
a small, undistinguished, clapboard building with one

of the big side windows smashed and glassless. Most of the posse carried on riding toward the saloon, but Scanlan and his two friends halted their horses in front of the county offices and dismounted. They swung up on to the sidewalk and watched Dickson's group dismount at the hitching rail.

"Mind if we come in with you, Jerome?" Scanlan asked. "Just to make sure the breed don't cut rough."

Dickson did not argue. He could hardly stop the three men entering his office after they'd ridden on the posse. He led the way through the double doors into the office of the county sheriff. The office was a large room with a desk in the center and a few chairs as furnishings. There was a stove in one corner and a big iron safe in another. The back of the office opened to the cells, but was separated from them by a set of folding doors which were open as the party entered. On one wall was a big cupboard and on the other side, facing it, a rack of rifles and shotguns. It was no different from any other sheriff's office, Dusty thought, looking around: the same worn desk, the same wanted posters. It might easily have been his father's office back in Polveroso City.

"I'll take the gunbelt, Mort," Dickson said. "Best hold you in the cell, too. Call it resisting arrest and damage to property."

"Sure, Jerome," Mort agreed, knowing the sheriff was only doing his duty.

Taking the gunbelt, Dickson put it and the broken revolver into the cupboard and took Mort into the cells, locking him inside the nearest. The other men waited in the office, none of them talking. The Ysabel Kid watched Scanlan, a mocking smile on his face, his yellow boy in his hands.

A big dog came through the door at the rear of the jail. It was a lean, gaunt and shaggy animal which looked to have more than its fair share of buffalo-wolf blood. With its long tail wagging it started forward

toward the cells and Mort Lewis came to the door,
grinning. The dog brushed against Scanlan's legs, barely
touching them, but the man snarled and drew back his
foot. Instantly, the dog leaped around, snarling low in
its throat. Scanlan's hand dropped. He brought the gun
out and fired, the heavy bullet smashing into the dog's
head.

The dog yelped once and went down. Dickson gave an
angry shout and started forward as Mort Lewis flung
himself at the bars of the cell. Dickson went at Scanlan
but fast as he moved, Dusty was faster.

Dusty hurled forward like a living projectile, his right
fist smashing into Scanlan's bristle-covered jaw. For a
small man Dusty was packed solid with steel-hard
muscles. He hit with every ounce of weight and strength
he'd got. Scanlan, taken by surprise both by the speed
of the attack and Dusty's unexpected strength, was
knocked staggering. He crashed in a sitting position
under the cupboard. Dusty came after him not letting
the other man get to his feet before attacking again.

Up drove Dusty's right hand in a brutal backhand
slam, the second knuckle catching Scanlan's top lip,
crushing and splitting it and sending waves of agony
welling through him. Dusty's hand swung up with the
force of the blow, then smashed down, driving into the
side of the man's face, snapping his head over. Scanlan
was unable to defend himself against the fury of the
attack. He was no mean hand in a roughhouse brawl but
this time was taken completely by surprise.

With an angry snarl, Milton jumped forward in an
attempt to help his friend. The lean man came fast, with
a wild rush which was calculated to take Dusty
unawares. Dusty's left hand shot up, jerked open the
cupboard and sent it smashing into the gunman's face.
Milton met it head on, the wooden edge of the door
smashing his nose. Before Milton could get up, and even
as his hand fell gunward and tears of pain half blinded
him, Dusty's right foot lashed up, kicking with the grace

of a French *savate* fighter. Caught in the middle of his
stomach by the high heel of a riding boot Milton
doubled over, his head narrowly missing the open cupboard door on the way down. Dusty's fist whipped up,
driving with all his strength. The knuckles caught
Milton's face as he bent over, jerking him erect. His
head smashed into the bottom edge of the door, splin-
tering the wood and tearing it from the hinges. The man
went limp and slumped to the floor, a passive look on
his face and a trickle of blood from his Stetson brim.

Salar let his hand fall to his side. No gentleman of
noble Spanish blood would sink to such a barbarous
practice as fist fighting. His hand was curling around
the ornate butt of his gun when he felt something resting
lightly on his wrist. All ideas of drawing the gun ended.
Resting on the wrist, just where the fancy white cuffs of
the shirt showed from the jacket sleeve, was the eleven-
and-a-half-inch-long, two-and-a-half-wide blade of the
Ysabel Kid's bowie knife, razor edge ready to rip home.
Slowly Salar looked up at the mocking red-hazel eyes of
the Ysabel Kid.

"I don't do no fist fighting, neither, Salar," warned
the Kid in a gentle tone which did not fool the Mexican.
"So leave her lie, afore I spoils them nice lace cuffs."

Salar removed his hand. He was proud of the lace
cuffs and did not want them torn, nor his wrist cut to
the bone.

Scanlan forced himself upward against the savage,
battering fists, bracing himself against the wall and
snarling threats through his bloody lips. He forgot his
gun, forgot everything, to get at this small Texan who
was smashing blows at him, rocking his head from side
to side. He got one foot into Dusty's stomach and
pushed hard, hurling him across the office. Dusty
slammed into the wall and bounced forward as, with a
roar of rage, Scanlan charged, meaning to smash Dusty
by brute strength.

For an instant Dickson thought he should help Dusty.

Standing transfixed, amazed by the strength of the small Texan and the fury of Dusty's attack, he saw the huge man charge and expected to see the small Texan smashed to the ground by sheer weight.

Dusty went straight forward, as if to meet the rush. At the last moment he swerved, caught Scanlan's wrist in his hands, and threw him at the wall. He was out of all control and crashed hard enough to jar the reward posters from their hook. Scanlan staggered back dazed but Dusty was on him again, turning him and sinking a fist almost wrist deep into his stomach. Scanlan croaked in pain and bent forward to meet the other punch Dusty was throwing, a beautiful left uppercut, timed to perfection to meet the downswinging jaw. The huge man was lifted erect, his arms flailing wildly as he went over and landed flat on his back.

Still Dusty had not finished. The sight of the dead dog, wantonly and needlessly killed, filled him with a cold and murderous rage. The Kid watched; he had never seen his friend so angry and hoped Dusty would remember that the deadly ju-jitsu and karate techniques, taught to him by Ole Devil Hardin's Japanese servant, could easily kill when used with full strength.

Gripping the front of Scanlan's shirt Dusty dragged the man into a sitting position and slammed home another punch, smashing his head to the floor. The big gunman was limp and unconscious but Dusty hardly noticed. He pulled the man half erect once more and his fist smashed home. He took hold of the shirt for another blow but Dickson decided it was time to intervene.

"Easy, Cap'n Fog," he said worriedly. "You'll kill him if you keep hitting him like that."

Slowly the anger left Dusty's eyes, the cold rage seeping out of him. He let go of Scanlan's shirt and the man flopped back limply to the ground. Then Dusty straightened up, his hands were clenched but he opened them, moving the fingers to get them working again. He was breathing heavily as he stepped clear of Scanlan and looked at the dog. Then his eyes went to Salar and there was cold, bitter hate in the gaze.

"Whose dog was it?" he asked.

"Mine," replied Mort Lewis and there was deep grief in his voice. "I've had him for years. He was about the only friend I ever had. If I get half a chance I'll kill Scanlan for doing that."

"He's not far from being dead now," Dickson put in grimly. "And, by gawd, he asked for it."

Dusty swung to face Salar. "Pick the dog up," he ordered.

"It is beneath the dignity of a—"

"Mister," Dusty's voice dropped to hardly more than a whisper. "You pick up that dog and carry it out of the door."

"And if I don't?" replied Salar.

The Ysabel Kid knew these race-proud Spanish Mexicans; they would rather die than submit to something beneath their dignity. Salar would willingly face Dusty with a gun, even if he knew he would die, rather than submit to an indignity. The knife point moved, dropping, and before Salar realized had slit the holster from top to bottom. Before the Mexican could move, his gun was gone, held by the Ysabel Kid. The Kid nodded to Dusty, knowing his friend could handle things.

"You'll either pick him up or I'll give you worse than I gave the other two."

For an instant Salar stood immobile. He could face death without flinching, risk his life for his perverted sense of honor. But he could not risk being beaten into a bloody, marked hulk like Scanlan. Salar was proud of his good looks; he would not risk having them battered by the hard fists of the small *Tejano*. There was hate and worse on the man's face as he walked forward and lifted the dog. He carried the dog out through the rear door of the jail and found there was worse to come.

"Get a shovel," Dusty ordered. "I want a grave digging."

Before Salar could decide if even a savage beating was worth the final and highest blow to his dignity there was an interruption. He was saved from making the choice by the Kid, who was looking out of the door.

"We've got us some trouble, Dusty," said the Kid. "Regular deputation for the sheriff. All righteous, upright and soberly solid citizens."

Dusty turned and walked back into the jail. Salar looked down at the dog, then at the loosened dog hairs which marked his elegant black coat. His hate for Dusty Fog grew by the minute, swelling to an almost maniacal rage. Then sense returned to him. He felt the slashed edges of the holster and knew his revenge would be delayed until he could get a new holster and make practice with it. He was fast with a gun, but only when drawn from a holster. He'd always used one and knew that any attempt at drawing from his waistband would be fatal for him. He must wait, have a new holster made, learn its hang and ways, and then take this accursed pair of *Tejanos* who had humiliated him.

The office was quiet as Dusty and the Kid went back. The Kid picked his rifle up, ignoring the two men who were just beginning to move. He glanced at the cell and gave Mort a reassuring nod, then joined Dusty at the side of the door, listening to what was going on outside.

The men out front were a mixed-looking bunch, a fair cross section of the town and county population. There were solid citizens wearing expensive or near expensive broadcloth jackets and the latest town-style trousers. There were cowhands from the local spreads, cheery, happy-go-lucky young men who were along to see what was happening. There were the saloon loafers who'd made up the posse and others of their kind. The rest were poor businessmen, trying to scratch a living in the town, a couple of poorly dressed professional gamblers and an odd assortment of less definable men, men who wore the cowhand dress, but were not cowhands, or Dusty did not know the signs.

The leaders of the deputation appeared to be a tall, handsome young man wearing expensive range clothes, a rangeland dandy, arrogant, successful and used to having his own way, and a shorter, thick-set townsman, the best dressed of the townsmen in the crowd. He was a pompous-looking, well-padded man, his side-whiskers and heavy moustache outward and visual proofs, as was his suit and the heavy gold watch chain across his vest, of his success and affluence.

The handsome man watched Dickson step from the office, glanced at the shotgun resting across the sheriff's arm and dropped his hand to fondle the butt of the pearl-handled Army Colt in his holster.

"You brought the half-breed in?" he asked, his voice tough, the voice of an important man dealing with an unimportant official.

"I brought Mort Lewis in," agreed Dickson.

"We've come for him, Jerome."

"There'll be no lynching, Stewart," warned Dickson.

"Lynching, sheriff?" Dave Stewart replied, looking indignant for the benefit of the crowd. "We don't aim to lynch him. We're going to give him a trial."

"Without a judge, or counsel for his defense?"

"Mr. Humboldt here's a justice of the peace, he can take the trial," Stewart scoffed. "We'll give the breed a fair trial, then hang him."

"Not so fast, David," the other man put in hastily. "We'll see he gets a fair trial, Jerome. Even a half-breed gets fair treatment in our town."

"I'm holding Mort for questioning, pending inquiry into Dexter Chass's killing," Dickson answered. "There's not enough evidence yet, not to bring a murder charge against Mort Lewis!''

"We'll be the judge of that," Stewart growled. "Won't we, boys?"

There was a low rumble of agreement from a section of the crowd. It was the starting rumble of a lynch mob but as yet not more than half of the men present would be willing to take the law into their own hands.

"Mort's held for questioning, nothing more. There'll be no trial."

Stewart smiled, his face hard and vicious. "You wouldn't be thinking of trying to stop us, would you, Jerome?"

"If I have to."

There was something in the way Dickson spoke which warned the men in the crowd that they would have to come openly against the sheriff if they wanted to take the prisoner. Many were willing to go along with the "trial" thereby gaining spurious legality for the proceedings. This same faction were not willing to gain even the good will of Dave Stewart and take the prisoner by force. Then the affair would carry the taint of a lynch mob and be against the law.

Dave Stewart knew the way the crowd was thinking. He knew that some of the loafers and hardcases would follow him, but they were not the people he must have behind him. He needed the support of the solid and influential citizens before he could stir up any outright attack on the sheriff; the support of the men who could cover the incident up after it was done. For their reputations and their necks, they would be compelled to keep quiet. He must go slowly, move the crowd gradually up to the point where they would not back down.

"Have it your way, Jerome," he said, knowing every man in the crowd was waiting on his words. "Folks feel bad about letting a half-breed kill a nice old man like Dexter Chass. Shoot him in the back and leave him out at his house like that. Why, old Dexter might have laid there for days, suffering, with the bullet in him and nobody'd have known. And you telling us that you're not going to let justice be done?''

''I'm telling you that I'm not satisfied that Mort's guilty.''

''What do you want? Him to admit it?'' Stewart replied. ''Let us talk to him for a spell. We'll soon get the truth out of him.''

''Mort stays where he is,'' Dickson answered.

''You wouldn't use that shotgun, not against your friends, Jerome,'' Stewart mocked. ''You aren't going to shoot down your good friends to save that—''

''Any man who tries to take a prisoner from me's no friend of mine,'' Dickson replied. ''You'd best break it up and go to your homes.''

''You're only one man, Jerome,'' warned Stewart. ''One man, a man the town appointed to defend them and their property from murderers like that half-breed. Now, one man's not going to stop us seeing justice done. Is he, boys?''

Put that way it was a challenge to the citizens; they had to stand up for their rights as freeborn Texans. They were mumbling among themselves, the more restless spirits preparing to take action. The odds were very good, one man against a crowd. Then the mumbles died as the jail door opened. It suddenly became more plain that it was three against the crowd.

Dusty stepped out, moving to Dickson's left side and stood with his hands resting at waist level, thumbs hooked in his belt. The Kid came out to the right side, looking meaner than hell. The old yellow boy held negligently in his right hand, the buttplate resting on his hip and the muzzle pointing into the air. His right hand moved, flipping open the lever and closing it again; then he stood without a move. His voice was cold and sardonic as he spoke to the crowd.

''Reckon you didn't take the trail count close enough, mister. Try again.''

''Who are they, Dickson?'' Stewart growled. He

could feel his hardcase, saloon loafers fading away from him, weakening before the two handy-looking men who flanked the sheriff. With men like that to back him, Dickson could inflict more than a little damage on the crowd.

"Captain Fog and the Ysabel Kid."

"Captain Fog," Stewart growled and the crowd repeated the names in a low rumble of sound. "You mean Dusty Fog?"

"As ever there was," replied the Kid, his mocking eyes on the rancher. "You gents still fixing to take the prisoner?"

Before Stewart could reply, the fattish, pompous-looking man by his side moved forward holding out his hand to Dusty trying to raise a welcoming smile which looked sincere.

"Captain Fog," he said, his unctuous voice full of respectful greeting. "My name is Humboldt. I believe your Uncle asked you to come and see me on his behalf?"

Dusty's hands stayed where they were; he made no attempt to take the proffered hand. "That's right. Uncle Devil sent me along to look into that idea of yours."

Humboldt coughed modestly. "I'm sure you'll find it most satisfactory—"

"What's all this about?" Dusty cut through the gushing words with his cold drawl. "You'd best tell it."

"Mort Lewis killed his neighbor," Humboldt replied. "We merely wanted to see that justice—"

"You sure he did it?" asked the Kid.

"- er - I—" Humboldt began, then faltered. It did not look as if Captain Fog and the Ysabel Kid approved of their actions, and they were two men he needed for the successful fulfillment of his plans.

"Sure we're sure," Stewart growled. "The breed's been feuding with poor old Dexter for years."

"You know what these half-breeds are, Cap'n,"

Humboldt went on, smiling ingratiatingly at the Kid. The dark young man was only an employee of Ole Devil Hardin but he was also reputed to be one of Captain Fog's closest friends. The small Texan might resent any snobbish objections to his friend, so the Kid rated very civil treatment. "You can't trust any man with Indian blood, can you?"

The mocking gleam in the Kid's eyes grew more in evidence. "Was the *hombre* scalped as well as shot?"

"Er – no. Not that I know of," replied Humboldt, clearly disappointed that he was unable to answer in the affirmative. "Why?"

"*You* know what Injuns are," grunted the Kid. "Course, the *hombre'd* only be half scalped, seeing as Mort's only half Injun."

The crowd watched the three men on the porch, the cowhands staring with admiring eyes at a master of their trade, a man they hero-worshipped. No cowhand would willingly go against the wishes of Dusty Fog. The rest of the crowd knew that there was no chance of their getting the prisoner and any attempt at doing so would be dangerous.

Humboldt licked his lips. He wanted to make a good impression on Dusty and said, "My house is, of course, at your disposal. I hope both you and the Kid will consider yourselves my guests."

"Not until this business is settled," replied Dusty. "Have you held an inquest on the killing?"

"Why, no, we haven't," replied Humboldt, brightening. Here was a way to settle this business without offending Captain Fog. Humboldt was sure that the young Texan would accept the evidence at its face value and there was much that was damaging to Mort Lewis. "I think we'd better do so, Sheriff."

"Yeah, it could do with a bit of airing," Dickson said dryly.

"Tell Warren we'll start in half an hour. Down at the Long Glass, Captain," he went on for Dusty's benefit.

Dusty nodded. There was nothing unusual in holding an inquest in a saloon. Often in a small town like Holbrock the saloon was the only place large enough for a court. The bar would be closed down and the inquest held in an air of sober respectability. Even ladies could enter the saloon at such a time, a thing never permitted under normal circumstances.

"It would be best," Humboldt managed to get a boom of civic righteousness in his voice. "After all, none of us wishes to take the law into his own hands."

The other townsmen, the more sober citizens of the crowd, gave their enthusiastic agreement to the words. None of them wished to become involved in a lynching. The Texas Rangers nosed out such things, no matter how well they were concealed. Somebody always talked and word got out. Once the Texas Rangers got to hear of the lynching, even as a drunken rumor, they would investigate and probe deeper until they got at the truth. Money, social position, local standing meant nothing to the Rangers when a crime had been committed. No man connected with the lynching would be safe again. So most townsmen were pleased that there was no immediate danger of lynching.

Stewart's face was hard, no longer smiling as he felt his support ebbing away. He wished he'd brought his ranch crew to town with him and wondered where Salar, Milton and Scanlan were. With them on hand he would chance facing the three men on the sidewalk before the jail.

The wish was partly granted. The jail door opened and Milton staggered out supporting Scanlan. Stewart stared, he could hardly believe his eyes at the sight. Milton's mouth was swollen and bruised, and there was a trickle of blood running from under his hat. He could barely stand, and the weight of Scanlan was making him stagger badly.

But Scanlan's condition was worse,. Stewart knew his foreman's skill as a roughhouse fighter and could hardly believe that he was seeing correctly. Scanlan's face was never anything to be proud of, but it looked far worse now. His top lip was swollen to almost four times its usual size, split and bloody; his right eye was slit and the rest of his face was marked to almost the same extent. Whoever had handled Scanlan in such a manner must, if lone handed, be a veritable giant, Stewart thought. He knew Dickson too well to think the sheriff had organized and helped in a mass attack on the two men.

"What the hell?" Stewart growled. "Who did that?"

"I did," Dusty replied.

It was on the tip of Stewart's tongue to snarl out a denial, but he saw that to do so would be tantamount to calling Dusty a liar. In Texas there was only one reply to such an accusation: a fast-drawn Colt.

"That's the living truth," Dickson went on. "Scanlan killed Mort's old Pete dog in there and Cap'n Fog took exception to it."

There sounded an angry, savage growl from the listening cowhands. Among the riders who worked around Holbrock the big dog was a firm favorite. It could outfight any other dog within miles and could run down a coyote, which no other dog could do. There'd been considerable money won betting on the dog in both capacities and the cowhands were riled by the wanton killing. If Mort Lewis himself had been killed by the posse, the cowhands would not have worried. He was one of them, friendly with them, but that was all. There would have been no demonstrations either for or against the man who had done the shooting. The dog was different and Stewart knew he'd lost the support of the cowhands for Scanlan was his man.

"You stood by and let him do that to one of my men?" Stewart snarled at the sheriff.

"That's right, I did," agreed Dickson evenly. "I'd have done it myself but Cap'n Fog licked me to it. You'd best get them to the doctor, Dave, happen you want to be on hand to give evidence.''

Stewart took the hint. He turned on his heel and a couple of the loafers helped his men to the doctor's house. The rest of the crowd began to move away. There was nothing more to be done now, except wait for the result of the inquest.

Humboldt and a couple of his partners moved forward. There was an air about all of them which amused the sheriff who knew them to be snobs of the first water. He knew that none of them would have thought of speaking to an insignificant looking cowhand like Dusty Fog unless there was something in it. They would have been even less friendly to the Kid under other circumstances, for there was a dangerous and most disrespectful air about him which would not go down with men like Humboldt.

"I hope that you'll find our little proposition quite to your satisfaction, Captain Fog," Humboldt gushed. "I'll expect you and your friend to dinner tonight, unless he'd rather I arranged alternative entertainment for him."

The Kid grinned. He knew that Humboldt would never think of inviting him to visit the house under normal circumstances and would have been only too keen to avoid the sort of dinner Humboldt would give. This time he intended to go along with Dusty, just for laughs.

"We'll see about it, after the hearing," Dusty replied. "I want to know what's happening hereabouts before I make any decisions."

"It's simple, really," Humboldt said. "Mort Lewis is a half-breed. He's supposed to run a small cattle spread in the hills but he spends a lot of time away from it. He acts as guide for hunting parties and things like that. His neighbor, old Dexter Chass, and he don't – didn't get on well together—"

"We'd best get to the Long Glass," Dickson put in.

"Will you and the Kid act as special deputies, Cap'n?"

"Sure will," Dusty agreed. "Go fetch that gent along, Lon."

The Long Glass saloon was quiet, soberly quiet. The bar and tables were cleared of glasses, bottles and decks of cards, and there was an air of expectancy among the all-male crowd, a silent awareness of dramatic happenings.

"If you'd care for a drink, to refresh yourself after your long ride, I think it could be arranged, Captain," Humboldt said in a confidential whisper.

"No thanks," Dusty replied, watching the door of the saloon. He saw the Kid approaching with Mort Lewis and glanced at Stewart who was sitting at a table at the side of the room.

Dickson took a seat at the same table as Dusty and Humboldt, in the center of the room. The Kid, still carrying his rifle, followed Mort to the bar just behind the table. Humboldt looked down at Mort, then gulped, for he was not fastened in any way. He was about to raise the matter when Dusty spoke:

"Start from the beginning, Sheriff. What's this all about?"

"Are you setting up as judge, or something?" Stewart asked.

"Nope, just wanting to hear why you want this man hung for a murder. Do *you* object, mister?"

Stewart's snort could have meant anything but he made no reply, nor did he offer to take up the challenge. He sat up straighter in his chair, his lips tight and unsmiling as he watched what was happening. Before the arrival of the small Texan, he would have been at that center table, running things. Now he was shoved back and the men who would have supported him were siding with Dusty Fog.

"First off, Captain," Dickson replied, speaking so that his words carried to the listening men. "Like you were told, Mort and Chass were neighbors. It's not good grazing up there in the hills and Mort allowed Chass was driving his stock on to the Lewis land. Got to hard words over it and Mort threatened to shoot any more of Chass's stock he found over the land."

"We all heard Lewis threaten old Dexter," Stewart yelled. "Right in this saloon he said he'd gun down any more of Dexter's cattle he found over the line. And shooting a man's cattle's a sure way to get him riled up and shooting back."

"Only there wasn't any shooting back, way you told it," Dusty answered. "What happened next, Sheriff?"

"Couple of days back, Dave there came in asking if anybody'd seen Dex Chass around. Nobody had, they'd not given it no thought, he didn't often come into town. So yesterday Dave went to see Chass and found him dead."

"That's right," Stewart put in. "He was lying face up. I didn't find the bullet hole until I went to look at him. He'd been shot in the back; been dead for ten, eleven days."

"How'd you know that?" Dusty asked, watching the rancher.

"I saw him eleven days back. Come to think of it, the date was the eleventh and it's the twenty-third today. Was over to talk a deal with Dex; he wanted to sell out, sounded real scared of Lewis. I told him to come over to my place and see me the next day but he never showed. We had that cloudburst, remember, Jerome? It kept me busy for the next few days and I thought Dex must have changed his mind. Then, when I heard nobody'd seen him around I went out to his place. He was either killed soon after I left or during the storm."

"You certain sure about the date?" inquired the Kid.

"I am. There were no tracks around the house and the rain left some real soft earth all around. The killing took place either before the storm, or during it; that was what washed the sign out. If it'd been done after the storm, there'd have been plenty of sign," Stewart replied.

"Was Chass good with a gun?" Dusty drawled.

"Naw," scoffed Stewart, seeing a chance to blacken the evidence against Mort Lewis even more. "Old Dex wasn't any sort of hand with a gun. Didn't even own a handgun, only a worn-out Kentucky rifle. He wouldn't have stood any kind of chance in a gunfight against the half-breed."

"That's strange."

"What's strange about it," growled the rancher, seeing Dusty was holding the crowd's attention.

"Why Mort'd shoot a man in the back and take a chance of getting hung, when he was in the right and could have taken the same man in what'd be classed as a fair fight," Dusty answered. "It doesn't figger to me."

"Hell, you all know what half-breeds are," Stewart answered. "He wouldn't stack up against any man in a fair fight."

"That's a lie and you know it, Stewart," Mort Lewis growled, he was quivering with anger but controlling it for he knew that if he attacked Stewart the rancher would shoot him down, pleading self-defense. "I'll face you any time you haven't got your hired guns at your back."

"Sounds like a fair offer," drawled the Kid. "Want the loan of my old Dragoon, Mort?"

"Cut it, Lon," barked Dusty. "Let this gent have his say, then we'll hear what Mort's got in answer to it. I haven't seen anything which makes me think that Mort did the killing."

"All right, I'll tell you why," Stewart replied. "I went across Lewis's land on the eleventh, looking for him. I saw about a dozen head of Chass's stuff over the Lewis line. I never saw a sign of Lewis but one of my boys reckoned he saw the breed skulking around the Chass place."

"One of your men?" Dusty put in. "How many did you have along?"

"Just a couple or so. Thought we might find some of my stock up there and be able to bring them down. It was Scanlan who thought he saw the breed."

"Did he see him?"

"Shem allowed he did," Stewart replied. "He could have come down after we'd gone and cut old Dex down."

"Who could have?" inquired Dusty mildy.

"Lewis. Who'd you think?"

"Way you said it, I'd have thought your man came back," Dusty drawled. "So you allowed that Mort must have done the killing. How about the body?"

"Brought it in with us, left it down at Doc Harvey's place for burial."

Dusty nodded. He turned in his chair and looked at Mort Lewis. "It looks like you'd best tell us where you were on the eleventh, Mort."

The young man frowned, then he looked relieved. "I wasn't anywhere near to Holbrook. I've been away for near three weeks."

"Where were you?" Dusty asked again.

"Took an Eastern newspaper woman and her artist out to Long Walker's camp."

"That sounds real likely!" Stewart yelled.

"Why shouldn't it be?" Mort answered. "I'm part Comanche and don't mind who knows it. Least, they never hold white blood against me. I took the young woman and this feller who done the drawings for her; they offered good money and I can always use that. Five days back I brought her out and down to Fort Worth, so's she could get a stage East with her story. When we got to Fort Worth she found that she'd left a book in the Comanche camp, one she used to write what happened each day in. Wanted me to go back for it, said she'd make it worth my while. I was going to head out when she said she'd heard from her paper; they wanted her to go some place and get another story. She paid me and told me to get the book, make it a package and mail it to the New York Tribune."

"And did you?" Humboldt asked, sounding as if he did not believe a word of what Mort had said.

"Came home first. I aimed to go out to my place, then make for Long Walker's village again."

"How about the woman?" Dusty put in. "What was her name?"

"Clover, Miss Anthea Clover, got it all down on a piece of paper in my warbag out to the spread."

"When did you get back?"

"Late afternoon, yesterday, Cap'n. I came into town this morning."

"Why'd you light out and run when the sheriff started to ask you about the killing?" Dusty went on.

"I saw Stewart and his boys watching. I didn't figure that anybody who counted would listen to me, or believe me. I didn't even figure I'd get a trial."

"Nonsense!" Humboldt barked. "I don't hold any man's blood against him. If the case came up—"

"I lit out as fast as I could, Cap'n," Mort interrupted. "You saw what happened when they caught up with me."

"I saw," agreed Dusty, then looked at Stewart. "Your men wanted to lynch Mort as soon as they caught up with him."

"Dex Chass was a real popular man."

"Was he?" Dusty drawled, his eyes on the rancher. "That still doesn't mean Mort killed him."

"Dex didn't have no enemies," growled Stewart.

"Knowed a real friendly man, one time," the Kid said. "Allus inviting folks into the house, feeding 'em and acting kind. Man he took in one night killed him for the bit of money he'd got."

"It's possible a stranger did the killing here," Humboldt put in, brightening slightly at the chance of getting Mort Lewis out of trouble without antagonizing Dave Stewart.

"Sure, there's no evidence that Mort did the killing. Only thing we know for sure is that he and Dex didn't get along," Dickson remarked. "And the same could be said about Dex and near on everybody he came in contact with."

"I daresay a good half of the town didn't really care for Dex at that," Humboldt said thoughtfully. "An unpleasant man, I always found."

The Ysabel Kid gave a laugh entirely without mirth. "Sounds like Mr. Chass wasn't so all-fired popular as we was led to believe. Half the town didn't cotton to him and he didn't have no enemies."

There was a guffaw of laughter from the cowhands. The Ysabel Kid had a reputation among them as a disrespecter of persons who would thumb his nose at the devil if he felt so inclined. Dusty Fog and Mark Counter might be regarded as tophands, and leaders of the cowland society, but the Kid was a wild heller with no respect for pomp and dignity. He was proving it here, for Stewart was a bad man to cross and should be accorded every respect.

"Reckon Dave gave us the wrong impression – unintentionally of course," the sheriff remarked, grinning broadly. "Ole Dex was a cantankerous, mean old cuss at best. He wouldn't get shot by anybody he took in for a meal, because he wouldn't offer to take them in in the first place. I don't reckon you could have found three people to give him a good word – afore he was killed."

"Got to be tolerable popular after he was dead," grunted the Kid. "But I still haven't seen anything to prove Mort did it."

"He ran away!" Stewart snapped.

"Sure, and he just told us why," Dusty replied evenly. "You and your crew would have been reaching

for a rope before Mort could open his mouth and tell
where he'd been.''

"Meaning?"

"You've been acting all-fired eager to get Mort
blamed and hung ever since he was brought in," Dusty
said, without raising his voice. "Why're you so eager?"
He paused, then went on. "It wouldn't be because
there'd be a chance of buying up two ranches, instead of
one?"

"I don't like the sound of that," Stewart snarled.

"Neither do I."

Stewart's eyes locked with Dusty's, but it was the
rancher who looked away first. He was faced down and
did not like the feeling, for he was the biggest rancher
around Holbrock. He'd also built up a reputation as a
fast-gun hardcase but knew he didn't stack knee-high
against that small, insignificant cowhand called Dusty
Fog. Stewart's ranch might seem big to Eastern eyes,
but the OD Connected, the spread where Dusty was
foreman, would swallow three ranches as big as
Stewart's. Stewart's outfit boasted they were tough,
hard and never curried below the knees, but the OD
Connected did not boast. They were acknowledged as
being without peer for salty toughness and Dusty Fog
was the toughest of them all. Scanlan's face was mute
testimony to that fact.

"All right," Stewart said finally. "I suppose you're
taking the breed at his word about not being around
here?"

"No, we're not," Dusty replied. "Where'd you stay
at Fort Worth, Mort?"

"Outside, sagehenning most all the time," Mort
answered. "I took Miss Clover in to the Bull's Head
Hotel, then moved out. Used to meet her on the edge of
town each day and show her what she wanted to see,
while she was waiting for the stage."

"She works for the New York Tribune," the sheriff

remarked. "Could they get word to her?"

"Sure, I reckon they might. She tells me she's been to other Injun villages. This new chore was to one out in the Dakota country. They might be able to get word to her."

"Which leaves that diary at Long Walker's camp," Dusty said thoughtfully. "That'd prove you'd been there, if it could be found."

"It's in my *tipi*," Mort replied.

"Which same means it'll still be there," the Kid went on. "It'll prove that you was there, I reckon."

"Who you got in mind to go and fetch it back?" Stewart growled. "Lewis? A white man'd be plumb loco to go in there."

"Sure would, Cap'n," a grizzled old-timer agreed. "Long Walker don't cotton none to white men going into his land. It's all right for young Mort there, he knows them."

Dusty smiled, then turned to the Ysabel Kid. "How about it."

"Dusty," replied the Kid, "you're looking at a real plumb loco man."

"There's no need for that, Captain," Humboldt spoke up. "We'll take Lewis's word for—"

"No you won't," Dusty barked. "Not just to keep on the right side of me. We aim to clear Mort, or find he's been lying."

Stewart grunted, coming to his feet. "So you aim to go and try to find Long Walker's camp, Kid?" he asked. "Hell, there ain't a *white* man in the state could do that."

"Waal, I'll surely give her a try," replied the Kid. "I'll be back by noon, seven days from now, Dusty."

"If you come back," Stewart sneered.

"I'll try, mister. I'll surely make a try."

"Then it's settled, gentlemen," Humboldt said, pleased that the inquest was over and hoping to get Dusty to talk business. "This inquest is postponed for seven days and will meet again at noon on the thirtieth to hear the evidence of the Ysabel Kid."

The bartender reached under the bar and brought out a bottle of whisky as a sign that the official business was over. The crowd made either for the door or the bar. Humboldt turned to Dusty, beaming with satisfaction.

"Would you care for that drink now, Captain?" he asked.

"Later, thanks. I'm acting as deputy for the sheriff and I've got to take the prisoner back to the jail."

"I thought you was so sure he was innocent," Stewart sneered. He'd come up and was near enough to have heard what Dusty had said.

"What difference does that make?" replied Dusty, and looked at Mort. "The sheriff's holding him on a charge of damage to property and he can't afford to pay either for the damage or his fine. Can you, Mort?"

"Sure can't, Cap'n," Mort answered. He did not know what Dusty was getting at but was willing to go along with it. "I'll just have to stop in jail until I can work it off."

Stewart did not reply. He could see what Dusty was doing. With Mort Lewis out of jail there was a chance of stirring up trouble, of pushing him into some foolish move. He turned and left the saloon, slamming through the batwing doors in a cold rage.

Humboldt rubbed his hands together. He was relieved that the Kid was to be away for a few days. He did not like the idea of that soft-drawling, mocking-eyed young man coming to his house. He was a wild cowhand and not the sort Humboldt would willingly invite. Being with Dusty Fog gave the Kid certain advantages but Humboldt was not sorry he was going. Now an offer to Captain Fog could be made; he could live at the Humboldt house instead of in the best room at the hotel as planned by Humboldt when he saw the Kid.

"My home is at your disposal, Captain," he said.

"Why, thanks, Mr. Humboldt. Trouble being I'm

still working for the sheriff and I'll be staying at the jail until the Kid comes back. We'll be ready to move in for a few days when he gets back.''

That was not what Humboldt had meant at all, but he did not say so. Before he was able to say anything more he was too late. Dusty, the sheriff and the Ysabel Kid had escorted Mort Lewis from the saloon and along the street to the jail. For a moment Humboldt stared at the swinging doors, then followed the others out, heading along the street.

Five hard-looking riders came into town, passing by the sheriff and throwing surprised glances at Mort Lewis. Dusty studied the men: they were not cowhands, even though they wore the clothes. Four looked to be experienced men in their late twenties and early thirties, but the other was a brash-looking youngster who would need watching. They passed on toward the other saloon, further along the street. Stewart was about to enter the saloon but stopped and waited for the men, saying something which made them look at Dusty's party with more interest.

"Stewart's bunch," Dickson remarked. "Calls them cowhands but I don't reckon any of them'd know a bull from a yearling heifer."

The Kid ran a hand along the neck of his white stallion. The horse snorted and swung its head to bite him. Grinning, the Kid gripped the saddle horn and swung afork his horse with a lithe bound. He looked down at the other three, then raised his hand in a mocking salute to Humboldt who was puffing along the street toward the jail.

"I'll see you in seven days at most, Dusty," he said. "Don't take any wooden nickels while I'm gone."

"Will you put the prisoner away, sheriff?" Dusty inquired. "I want to go out to the Chass place, happen you can find me a guide."

"Reckon Humboldt'd be more'n pleased to show you the way, only he doesn't know it," Dickson replied, grinning broadly, looking at Humboldt, deep in conversation with one of his cronies. "He must think a tolerable piece about you, way he acted to the Kid."

"Could be our charm," drawled Dusty. "Or the fact he wants Uncle Devil to sink some money into an idea he's got. One thing, though, the name's Dusty."

"Best call me Jerome, though why my pappy wanted to tie me with a handle like that I'll never know. Might be he was trying to get revenge on me for keeping him awake for the first three weeks I was born. I'd like to go out to the Chass place with you, but one of us had best stop in town and watch out for Mort."

"Be best," Dusty agreed.

A cowhand left the Long Glass saloon, mounted his horse and rode slowly along the street. From the dejected way he slouched in the saddle it was plain to both Dusty and Dickson what was wrong.

"Howdy, Wally," Dickson greeted. "You spent your pay already?"

"Waal, not exactly," replied the cowhand. "Don't you ever draw one card to an inside straight, Jerome. Or if you do, don't bet on it when the other man stands pat. You cain't win."

It explained why Wally was heading back to his ranch. He'd lost his pay trying to fit a card into the center of a running sequence at poker, a thing not advocated by the most skilled players.

"Like to earn five dollars?" Dusty asked.

"Depends who I've got to kill," grinned Wally.

"Nobody. I've got a herd of sheep outside town. Wants a man to care for them."

"*Sheep!*" Wally bellowed. "Me, tending damned woolies?"

"All right then," Dusty answered, showing nothing of the amusement he felt. "If you don't want that chore, how about taking me out to the Chass place?"

"Don't know as how I wouldn't herd sheep," grunted Wally. "All right, Cap'n, you hired yourself a

man. Wally's tours of the old West, see the sights of
Holbrock County, smell the rare, sweet-scented Chass
place. You want to go out to it right now?''

"Just one call to make," replied Dusty.

Dickson took Mort to the cells and placed him in one,
not bothering to lock the door; then returned to Dusty.
He looked at the small Texan and asked:

"Do you believe Mort's story?"

"Sure. It'd have to be true. A man lying'd make up a
better story than that."

With this Dusty turned and with Wally by his side
rode slowly along the street. At the Bella Union saloon
he halted his horse. This was the second of Holbrock's
saloons and Stewart was inside. Dusty left his horse at
the sidewalk and with Wally on his heels went inside.

Stewart looked up as Dusty entered. The rest of his
men were seated at the table and all flashed looks at the
youngest member of their group. The youngster grinned
back and dropped his hand to loosen his gun. He'd been
laughing at Salar for failing to take Dusty Fog and
boasting what he would do if given the chance. Now it
would appear his chance was on hand. He was primed
for trouble, egged on by the rancher and the other men.

Halting at the table Dusty looked at the rancher and
spoke, his voice carrying to every man in the saloon.

"Mr. Stewart, I'm riding out of town for a spell.
When I come back I'll expect to find Mort Lewis alive
and well."

"And what if he isn't?"

"I'll kill you on sight."

The words were spoken with complete assurance.
Stewart's face lost some color and he tried to keep his
voice hard as he growled:

"I wouldn't want to think you're threatening me."

"Why not?" replied Dusty. "That's just what I'm
doing."

"Hold i—!" began the young gunman, starting to his
feet.

Then he stopped, halfway up, his chair scraping back behind him. He looked as if he'd turn to stone. Dusty's hands had crossed, made a sight-defying flicker of movement and both matched guns were out, lined, the hammers drawn back to set lead flying. It took him barely half a second from the start of the move to reach his position of readiness.

"Sit down!" Dusty's drawl cut like a knife, sending the youngster back to his seat. The matched guns seemed to be picking out every man at the table, choosing each one as the first mark. "What I said goes, Stewart," Dusty went on. "Remember it. And the next time don't have a green button to do your fighting for you."

With that the guns went back to leather and Dusty turned contemptuously out of the saloon. Wally stood with his mouth hanging open, not knowing what to make of the scene, then followed Dusty out. Not a man at Stewart's table made a move; they hardly appeared to breathe until the doors swung closed on Dusty. Then Stewart let out his breath in a long sigh and looked at the others. His face was pale under the tan.

"What now, boss?" asked the biggest of the men, a hardcase called Smith.

"Leave Lewis alone. Dusty Fog's got friends. They'd be here if anything was to happen to that short runt. We'll wait for the trial, there'll be enough on the breed to convict him. I'll send to Lawyer Rollinson from Dallas to come and prosecute. He'll get Lewis tried and convicted for us."

"I don't know, boss," Smith replied. "You told us about that diary. Mort Lewis would've made a better story'n that if it warn't true."

"Sure," agreed Stewart, looking thoughtfully at the others. "Do you reckon the Ysabel Kid could find that Comanche camp?"

There was no reply for a moment, then Salar spoke: "I've seen the way the Kid walks, way he rides a hoss, way he talks, way he looks at a man. He's Indian enough to find it.''

"Then get after him!" Stewart snapped. "All of you. Get him, Salar."

"How do you want him, *señor*?"

"Dead! If you get him near the Comanche lands make it look as if they killed him. But get him one way or another."

Dusty and the young cowhand made good time to the Chass place. It was a small, untidy, badly cared for building, the windows covered with dirty sacks. The moment Dusty came near enough he could see why Wally did not care for the place. The stench of dirt and decay of rotting food and filth pervaded the air and almost masked the sickly smell of death.

The house was just as dirty as Dusty had expected from outside appearances. It was just a one-room building and was filthy beyond belief. The furnishings were poor and rickety; the table lay on one side and a chair sat broken in a corner. Dusty went in, his face wrinkling with distaste. He struck a match and looked around; there was no need to search the man's belongings. Dusty was looking for more than clothing or gear, something he could not explain. He'd a hunch about this business; something said at the inquest had caught his attention and he wanted to check his theory.

"Hold the door open, Wally," Dusty said, ripping the sacks from the window as he spoke to let more light into the room. "I want to look at the floor."

Dusty examined the floor; there was a shape marked out in the dust and dirt, the shape of a human body. It was blurred and indistinct but told him all he wanted to know.

Turning, he walked to the door. Wally stood outside. "Back to town now, Cap'n?" he asked.

"I'd like to see the Lewis place first." Dusty replied.

"Would we have time afore nightfall?"

"Be dark afore we get back to town," Wally replied.

"See you get double time after midnight," grinned Dusty. "It's a funny thing about the blood, Wally."

"I didn't see no blood."

"Yeah. That's what's funny about it."

They rode on across country, forded a shallow stream and reached the Lewis place as the sun was setting. Mort's house was no bigger, although better cared for, than the other cabin. As they rode up, Dusty noticed that there was only one set of tracks but he could not tell anything about them. He was not skilled at reading tracks and wished he'd got the Kid along. To the Ysabel Kid they would have told a complete story. It was the same at the other place; there was a sign, but Dusty could not tell if it was recently made or not.

The inside of the house was fairly clean. A warbag was lying on the bed and Dusty took it up. He opened the neck and tipped the contents out. The first thing he saw was a slip of paper. He opened it and red Miss Anthea Clover's name and address, written in a neat, feminine-looking hand; that proved part of Mort's story and should be enough to clear him, for they could find the woman and get her evidence. There was Mort's spare clothing in the bag and a powder flask, bullet-bag and bullet mold. Dusty picked up the bullet mold and examined it. It was the same as the one Dusty used and looked like a nutcracker except the crushing end was solid in two pieces, with two small holes in the center. The two holes allowed the molten lead for the bullets to be poured into the molds inside the metal end. Dusty opened it and noticed something straight away. The two molds allowed a man to make either round ball or the conical, elongated bullets which were used as a load for the Colt 1860 Army revolver. But with this one, only round balls could be made; the elongated mold was broken through at the pointed end and would be no use.

Putting the rest of the gear into the warbag, Dusty shoved the mold into his pocket and went to the door. Wally stretched and yawned showily, then grinned and mounted his horse. Dusty swung afork the paint and they rode away from the cabin, heading for town.

The clock was touching ten when Dusty rode up to the corral which formed the civic pound and the sheriff's stable. It was empty, so Dusty turned his horse in through the gate. He cared for the big stallion, paid off Wally and then went to the jail. Mort Lewis and Dickson were playing checkers in the office when Dusty came in.

"See all you wanted to, Dusty?" Dickson asked.

"Sure," agreed Dusty, going to the cupboard and taking Mort's revolver out. He looked down the chamber front, seeing the round heads of the .44 balls used for the load. Taking the mold from his pocket he went on. "How long's the conical shaper been broken, Mort?"

"Shucks, six month or more. I dropped the damned thing and a piece broke out of it. Would have writ and complained to Colonel Colt but I never used the shaped bullets anyway."

"You're like the Kid – pour a load in raw and stick a round ball on top?"

"Sure. I tried the combustible cartridges one time but the charge in them's too light."

Dusty replaced the gun, his face showing nothing of the interest he felt. He came to the table and moved one of Dickson's men to another square, allowing Mort to clear the board in a series of jumps.

"Why'n't you go out and look up Mr. Humboldt?" Dickson growled. "He's been here about every ten minutes, wanting to know if you're back."

"I'll likely do just that," replied Dusty. "Who's your coroner?"

"Doc Harvey. Doctor and undertaker both. He gets them coming and going."

"Let's go see him," suggested Dusty. "Shut your cell door as you go in, Mort."

The sheriff rose and followed Dusty from the office.

Mort rose, cleaned the checkers, cigarette butts, burnt matches and coffee cups from the table. Then he turned and went back to his cell, closing the door behind him and lying on the hard bunk.

The doctor was annoyed at being called into his office at half past ten. He was a thin, miserable-looking man wearing a sober black suit, a white shirt without a collar and slippers. His pleasure was even less as he listened to the reason for the visit.

"Sure, I shoved old Dexter under as fast as I could get the hole dug," he grinned. "Did it as fast as I could."

"You examine the body, doctor?" asked Dusty.

"Nope. He'd been dead at least eleven days. It wouldn't have been a pleasant chore."

"It won't get any better either," Dusty replied gently. "Sheriff wants him out and the bullet dug out before morning."

"What!" Harvey howled like a stuck goat at the words. "I can't rightly do that. I buried him—"

"And you're going to have to dig him up again," Dickson replied. You're county coroner, Doc, and get paid for handling things like this. There's been some talk around the county commissioners' about stopping paying you as there's not been any work for you to do."

"He's buried proper. I don't reckon I could dig him up without an order from the Justice of the Peace."

"All right, Doc," Dickson answered mildly. "I'll go see Mr. Humboldt now. He was asking me if I'd found out where that fifty-dollar consignment of coroner's gear had gone. Saw Big Maisie down to the Flats yesterday. She's got a necklace that looks like it cost all of fifty dollars."

Harvey's sallow face looked even paler. He shot a nervous glance at the door which led to his living room. "Hold your voice down, Jerome," he ordered quickly. "You know there ain't nothing in that story. It's just that the wife wouldn't understand and I hates to see her worried. When do you want the bullet?"

"We'll lend you a hand," Dickson replied.

"Doc," Dusty remarked as the men left the room, heading for the graveyard. "It's right you can tell which way a body was lying by where the body blood's settled down, isn't it?"

"I heard something about it," Harvey growled back. "See, Jerome, the blood clots down. If he's been lying on his stomach it settles in the front or vice versa."

Dickson nodded. He knew how blood settled and wondered if the doctor had made any of the tests he was supposed to as coroner. It was understandable if he had not, Dickson decided, as they uncovered the coffin, raised it to the surface and opened the lid. Harvey, muttering miserably, pulled a bandana over his face and went to work.

Dusty and Dickson drew back, allowing him to work, and stood in silence. Then they replaced the body and reburied it in the shallow grave. Harvey licked his lips nervously and held out his hand with a piece of lead in it.

"Here you are, Jerome," he said "This's the bullet. He'd been lying on his back, from all the signs."

Dickson struck a match and looked at the bullet. It was elongated, the tip just a little bushed by the impact with flesh. Dusty took the bullet and nodded as if he'd been expecting it.

"Thanks, Doc," Dickson said.

"That's all right," Harvey answered. "Er – Jerome – about that fifty-dollar consignment that was lost!"

"I don't know a thing about it, Doc," the sheriff drawled. "Send me a written report of what you found."

The doctor went his way, leaving Dusty and Dickson to go toward the jail. The sheriff watched Dusty, then remembered something that was bothering him.

"Stewart's men left town soon after you did."

"So?"

"They were headed out the same way as the Kid."

"Likely. I thought they might. Keep them out of our way," drawled Dusty.

"What'd you find out at the Chass place?"

"Nothing much. Only that Chass wasn't killed in the house at all."

Dickson stopped, his worries about the Ysabel Kid fading as he faced Dusty. "What did you say?"

"Chass wasn't killed in the house. He was lying on his back, according to the doctor and Stewart. But there was no blood on the cabin floor. The bullet was still inside, too."

"So what?"

"Chass lived in a small cabin. Had he been shot across the width of it, the bullet would have gone clear through him. He was lying in the center of the room, so the bullet should have gone through. It didn't."

"You know something?" Dickson growled.

"Nope. Suspect a mite but I'm not talking about it, yet."

They walked on together and at the jail Dickson stopped. "Dusty! There's six men after the Kid. Stewart's boys must be looking for him."

"Likely," agreed Dusty, sounding unconcerned.

"What's Stewart playing at?" growled Dickson. "Why's he want Mort killed, or the Kid for that?"

"I don't know about Stewart unless he wants the Lewis place as well as Chass'. In that case he wouldn't want the Kid to come back with proof that Mort was at the Injun camp."

"I'll jail him first thing tomorrow," Dickson snapped.

"And he'd walk out as soon as he'd got a lawyer," drawled Dusty. "We've no proof that Stewart's men went after the Kid."

"Aren't you worried?"

"Sure, they might catch up with Lon. That'd be real dangerous."

"Sure it would. The Kid—"

"I mean dangerous for them," replied Dusty, with complete confidence in his friend's ability to take care of himself. "How'd you like to come to the Humboldt house for lunch tomorrow?"

"I'm not likely to get invited, not until nearer election time," Dickson answered with a grin.

Dusty grinned back. "You wouldn't want to bet on that?"

The Ysabel Kid turned in the saddle of his big white stallion and looked back across the range. The woods were well behind him now and he was headed through the rolling, broken, open range country. He gave the land behind him a thorough scrutiny, missing nothing, not even the small cloud of dust some two miles behind him. It was a small cloud for the ground did not give off much dust and a less keen-eyed man might have missed it, but not the Kid. One horse could not cause so much dust-stirring, that was for sure.

Equally for sure, the riders were following him. He'd changed direction twice since first discovering he was being followed and each time the dust cloud had changed where he'd turned.

"Still coming, old Nigger hoss," he said, with quiet satisfaction. "They got a man with 'em as can read sign. Waal, we can make that same sign – and hide it some, too."

The pursuit did not unduly worry the Kid. The men were a good two miles behind him and traveling slower, reading his sign. While they were following him, the Kid was making more tracks ahead of them. It would be dark soon and the Kid knew he was in no danger. He would make a dry camp ahead and they would never find him in the darkness. There was no chance of the men riding up on him; his senses were too alert for that. There was no chance of their finding him by accident; his horse was trained to remain silent at such times; a thing of great use to a man when he was smuggling, and hiding in the dark from the contraband-hunting Border Patrol.

He twisted back and slouched easily in the saddle, allowing the big horse to make a gentle pace across country. He was out in the open and the men might be able to see him but that was no danger. They could not run him down before it was dark and would only tire their horses trying, while he could hold this even walk and keep the white stallion fresh for a run if they closed with him. The men would know this and would keep to his tracks, trying to avoid being seen. If they knew the country they'd head for a waterhole or stream near to the Kid, working on the assumption that he would camp near water.

Just before darkness the Kid found a stream, watered his big horse, filled his canteen, then rode on for another mile before making a dry camp. He was indifferent to hardship and just as at home sagehenning under the stars as in a bed at the OD Connected ranch house. He ate some hardtack from his saddlebag, drank sparingly, and cared for his horse; then with his saddle for a pillow and his old yellow boy close to hand, the Kid went to sleep.

His guess proved correct. Salar and his men made for the stream, reaching it in the darkness, and tried to locate his camp. They gave up the attempt in the end and went to sleep, waiting for the morning when they hoped to relocate the Kid's tracks. It would cause a considerable delay.

Before dawn the Kid, refreshed by a good sleep, was riding on. He estimated that he'd increased his lead on the pursuing men and still knew a trick or two to confuse them. The man who was reading sign back there was good and would be hard to throw off the track. Then the Kid remembered that Salar was known as a skilled reader of sign.

The Kid thought of this as he rode on, keeping his eyes open for a certain type of country. He had to prevent the other men from getting too close now. Salar was known as a fine rifle shot and there'd been a Buffalo Sharps rifle in the Mexican's saddleboot when he rode with the posse. If Salar was to get within half a mile of the Kid and find a clear shot it was doubtful if the Kid would know what had hit him.

Luck favored him for just ahead he saw what he wanted, an arroyo. He rode toward the steep sloped gash where rains and flowing water had eroded the land, biting down deeper and deeper until the slopes were over ten feet high. The Kid hoped the bottom would be a fast-flowing stream over hard rock but found instead there was no water at all. The rains of almost a fortnight earlier had swept along the arroyo bottom, leveling the sandy soil and leaving it soft. A horse would leave plain tracks down there, marks which a half-blind Digger Indian could follow.

Curiously, the Kid was not overly disappointed at the sight. He turned in his saddle and, while the horse picked a way along the edge of the arroyo, unstrapped his bedroll and got two blankets out. He saw a place ahead where the steep slopes were cut back to allow an easy way down in the bed of the arroyo. Before turning the big white stallion the Kid gave the surrounding land a careful glance. The men following behind must be at least three or four miles back and traveling slow. They were nowhere in sight and he doubted if they could see him.

The horse knew what to expect and halted at the top of the slope. The Kid dismounted and spread the two blankets end to end, down the slope. The horse stepped on to the blankets, walking forward over the first, and halted before leaving the second.

The Kid worked fast. He brushed away any signs of his progress and lifted the first blanket, carrying it ahead of the second. The white moved forward and the process was repeated. Each time the Kid moved a blanket forward the horse stepped on to it. Even on the soft sand of the arroyo bottom the horse's weight was distributed and there was no sign of its passing.

It was slow work; the Kid turned downstream, in the opposite direction to which he wanted to go. For almost half a mile he followed the base of the arroyo until he found a place to leave. He'd passed other places but hoped the men trailing him were going to have some trouble in locating which way he'd gone.

Reaching the top of the arroyo the Kid made sure his departure was not too obvious. Then, rolling the blankets once more, he headed across country. Now he kept to every bit of cover he could find, sticking to low ground and never crossing a rim without making a searching examination of the surrounding land.

Eventually he reached a spot where he could not keep hidden, he had to ride across nearly half a mile of open land. The big white stallion, with the Kid dressed all in black, would stand out like a nigger on a snowbank. A man on a high place miles back might see him and that would spoil all his work in the arroyo. The riders would head for the spot, then find his tracks.

Stopping his horse in the shade of a clump of scrub-oaks, the Kid dismounted and opened his warbag. He took out a light grey shirt and a pair of blue jeans, then changed into them. Next he took a package from the warbag, placed his black shirt and trousers in and turned back to the horse. The Kid opened the package and dropped a hand into it looking at the black powder which was smeared on his fingers. He rubbed his hand along the horse's neck and watched the black mark left behind. Working fast the Kid turned his white into what appeared to be a piebald. Then, packing his gear, he fixed it to the saddle and rode forward into the open.

Far behind, riding the trail left by the Kid, Salar and the other five men were worried. They'd failed to find where he had camped on the previous night and had wasted time trying to locate his tracks the following morning. The gunmen did not like the way things were going. The Ysabel Kid apparently knew they were after him and if he decided to make a fight of it they must see him first or some of them would be dead.

Ahead of the others, riding slowly and watching the ground all the time, was Salar. There was enough sign for him to be able to follow the Kid without any great trouble, but he knew he was dealing with a man who knew much both at following and hiding his trail.

Suddenly Salar brought his horse to a halt. The tracks they'd been following along the top of the arroyo were no longer to be seen. He halted and stared at the ground. Swinging from his horse be bent closer, his eyes examining every inch of the earth before him.

"What's wrong, Salar," Smith asked.

"The Kid's playing clever," Salar replied, looking around him.

The young gunman, eager to make up for his failure with Dusty Fog at Holbrock, rode to the end of the arroyo and looked down. "He never went down there," he announced. "It's clear, ain't no sign of a track."

Salar stepped forward, his eyes on the gentler slope which led to the bottom of the arroyo. There was a twisted smile on his lips; he knew what the Kid had done. It was going to take some hard work to find out in which direction the Kid had gone and even more to know where he had left. Salar knew that he was matched by a man who knew as much about tracking as he did himself. He also got the feeling the Ysabel Kid knew who was doing the trailing.

"One thing's for sure," Smith growled. "He didn't take wing and fly off."

"That's right, he did not," agreed Salar. "I know what he did, the blanket trick. I wondered when he would try to throw us. We'll have to try and find where he left."

"On the other side most likely," Smith suggested.

"Most likely, but not certainly. The Kid knows we're after him and he might come up this side again, then follow the arroyo until he can cross without our seeing his sign."

"What are you fixing to do, Salar?" asked one of the other men.

"Go down to the bottom and find out where the Kid left. It's going to take some time."

Smith slouched in his saddle and fumed at the delay. The Kid was ahead and still covering ground. If there'd been a point high enough one of the men could have tried to see some sign of the dark boy on the white horse. It would have been possible to spot them a good distance away. But there was no piece of land high enough for them to make use of it.

So the gunmen waited, resting their horses while Salar made a careful search. It took the Mexican all of an hour and a half to locate where the Kid had left the arroyo and pick up the trail. Salar could not hurry: the Kid knew they were after him and was taking some trouble to make his line as awkward as he could.

At last Salar brought his horse to a halt. He sat looking round him, remembering just where he was. Smith watched the Mexican and asked:

"What's holding us up now?"

"I have a – what you call it – hunch," Salar replied. "The Kid's making for Sanchez Riley's place."

"Could be at that," agreed Smith. Sanchez Riley's store-saloon-hotel lay near the edge of Comanche country. The gunman knew of the place, but had no idea where it was. "If he hasn't we'll have lost him for good."

"We have now," reminded Salar. "He's got such a lead on us that he'll be over the Salt Fork of the Brazos and into Comanche country. I don't think we'll follow him over the river."

Neither did Smith. It would be highly dangerous for a white man, or a party of white men, to enter the domain of the Comanches. There was much to be said for heading for Sanchez Riley's place. The man knew what

went on in the Comanche country and might hear if the
Kid slipped in. There was also a chance the Kid would
stop off at Sanchez Riley's and they might catch up with
him there.

"Let's head for Riley's, then," grunted Smith. "How
come you know where it lays, Salar?"

"I worked up this way once before," replied the
Mexican, but did not say who he had worked for or
what he had done. "I know the way."

It was night as the Ysabel Kid rode toward Sanchez
Riley's place. There was only one light showing in the
big T-shaped building which housed a store, a saloon
and a hotel. He was almost to the building when he
remembered something which made him worried about
his decision to come this way.

"Damn it, Nigger hoss," the Kid said, as he rode
nearer the three big corrals a short way from the
building. "I done forgot ole Salar used to ride for
Thomas Riveros' Comanchero bunch. He'll know how
to find this place. Us'ns best sleep easy."

The horses in the corrals moved around. In two of the
corrals were several animals; the Kid looked them over
with care. In the first corral were Sanchez Riley's
horses; in the second, some half dozen or so really
fine-looking animals. The Kid studied them; they were
good, fast stock, better than the average cowhand
would be riding. Such horses would be owned either by
a party of Texas Rangers or a bunch of outlaws. One
was as likely as the other to be staying at the house.

In the other corral there was only one horse. The Kid
looked at it and a grin split his face, his teeth showing
white against his dark skin. The horse was a white, a
fine looking animal and almost as large as the Kid's
Nigger. Seeing it gave the Kid another idea. He'd meant
to leave his horse in a corral if one was empty, but not
now.

About a hundred yards from the building was a large
clump of scrub oaks. The white could stay there; it

would find plenty of good grazing and water and would not stray. The Kid headed to the clump, removed the saddle and laid it carefully in the protective cover of a thick bush, leaving his rifle in the boot. Earlier in the day he'd washed the black coloring from the horse and resumed his normal clothing. Now he was pleased he'd done so. The black clothing merged into the darkness and he could move on silent feet, almost invisible in the night.

The light came from the dining room on the hotel side of the building and was the only part of the big house which showed any sign of life. The Kid made for one of the two doors but took the precaution of looking through the window before entering the room.

A big, fattish man and a tall, slender, black-haired girl sat at a table, but they were the only occupants. The Kid relaxed, pushing open the door and walking in.

For one so fat-looking, the big man was not slow. He came to his feet as the door opened, a Dragoon Colt lined on it. He was a cheery-looking man, his face a mixture of Spanish and Irish blood. He wore a dirty white shirt, open at the neck, cavalry blue trousers and his feet were bare. Yet there was nothing dirty or unkempt about him.

"*Cabrito*!" the man yelled, lowering the gun, as he recognized an old friend. "Long time since we was seeing you last."

"Howdy, Sanchez," replied the Kid, holding out his hand to the man. "You get fatter every time I see you."

"Tis praising me you are," Riley said, his voice seemed to be warring between the brogue of old Ireland and the gentler accents of Spain.

The girl was also on her feet. She was pretty and tall and her sleek black hair was as dark as the Kid's own. She was dark-eyed and there was something wild about her which might have resulted from her Comanche mother. She was Rosita Kathleen Riley, the big man's only child.

"*Hola Cabrito*," she said, coming forward with her arms held out to the Kid. Then in Comanche she went on, "And how many girls have you kissed since we last met?"

"Not one, Little Bird," replied the Kid, speaking Comanche just as faultlessly, then returning to English again. "I've got to be going on tomorrow, good and early, Rosie gal."

"Huh!" she pouted. "I bet you're going to see another girl. You and that big, white-haired gringo, Mark Counter, there's not the one a girl might trust."

The Kid laughed. Sanchez Riley's daughter would not speak to any other man in this manner. No other man could have come in and kissed her without her father to contend with, but the Kid was exceptional. He ruffled the girl's long hair, then turned his attention to Riley:

"You all got a room, Sanchez?"

The big man shook his head, looking distressed. "*Cabrito*, son of my oldest and best friend, I must tell you I have not. All my six bedrooms are being used by guests. Would you care to share my room?"

"No thanks. I'll be lighting out early and don't want to disturb you. Say, Rosie, how about some food? Then I'll bunk down here on one of the tables."

The Kid was mildly curious about the guests who'd taken all Riley's bedrooms but he did not ask. The men were most likely outlaws either going to or coming from a job and curiosity about such might only bring trouble. A man's private business was his own, so the Kid asked no questions.

The girl flitted into the kitchen and came out with a plate of stew. The Kid sat at a table and ate with the appetite of a healthy young man. He ate well, and drank the coffee the girl brought, for he did not know when he would get another meal.

While the Kid was eating, Riley sat with him, bemoaning the poor quality of the Rio Grande smugglers and comparing them unfavorably with the

Kid's father, Sam Ysabel. To Sanchez, it was cheaper to buy the goods legally than from the men who now ran contraband across the big river.

"It was a terrible blow when you retired, *Cabrito*," he finished.

"You could be right at that," grinned the Kid. He might have been a successful and prosperous smuggler had he not thrown his lot in with Dusty Fog after the death of Sam Ysabel. There were times when the Kid missed the thrill of running smuggled goods, but they were very rare. His life at the OD Connected, as a member of Ole Devil's floating outfit, was rarely dull enough for him to have time to spare in fruitless daydreaming.

"I wish you'd take my room, old friend."

"No thanks, Sanchez. I might have some callers looking for me and I don't want you getting into no fuss."

Sanchez Riley snorted angrily. "Your father and I went into the Comanche country as friends. If you are in any trouble—"

"I'm not. There's a bunch after me but I might have shook them. I left my old Nigger hoss out back there. Saw a white in the corral, who's it belong to?"

"Rosita. Long Walker sent it to her as a birthday present," Riley replied, a worried note in his voice. "I'm a mite unsettled about having it."

"Why?"

"It's got a 7th Cavalry brand on it."

"That's that loud mouthed Yankee General Custer or something they call him, he runs the 7th," the Kid replied. "He still pushing trouble, like last year on the Washita at Black Kettle's village?"

"Sure, got his patrols crossing into the Comanche lands."

The Kid grunted angrily. Men like Custer were a menace to the peace of the West. They repeatedly broke the peace-treaties other men had risked much to make with the hostile Indian tribes. This infringement on the land of the Comanche would make the other shore of the Brazos River's Salt Fork unhealthy for the white man. There was only one bright spot about the whole business: it would be likely to halt any further pursuit of him.

"One of these days that loud-mouthed, long-haired Yankee's going to learn what a riled, hostile Injun can do," the Kid prophesied, and his guess was to be proved correct in a few years time on the banks of the Little Bighorn River.

Rosita returned, carrying a couple of blankets and a pillow. She put them on the table, then went to blow out all but one small lamp which stood on the mantle over the fireplace. The Kid poked the pillow with a finger, tossed his hat on to the table and grinned at the girl; he looked about fourteen years old in the light of the lamp, but Rosita was not fooled. She knew that here was as dangerous a *man* as could be found anywhere in the West.

"That's a tolerable hard pillow you've given me, gal," he said.

"Hard like your heart, *Cabrito*," she answered in Comanche. "Sleep well."

"And you. Sleep deep and dream happy."

Riley and his daughter left the Kid alone in the dining room and he put the pillow at the edge of the center table. It would be a good deal softer than the saddle which he would be using for the next few days. He drew the blankets up around his ears, slid his hat to one side of his head, and went to sleep. The Kid could sleep anywhere, any time, and not even the faint lamp glow could keep him awake.

The lamp was left for a purpose. If a chance traveler came on the building in the dark he could enter the dining room and sleep on one of the tables, or the floor, without waking Riley or any of the other guests. This was the reason the Kid took the center table; anybody coming in could use one nearer the door without having to disturb him. There was another reason: anyone trying to sneak up on the Kid would have a longer walk, giving more warning noise to his keen ears.

Six riders came slowly through the darkness toward Sanchez Riley's place, slouched in the saddles like tired men, their horses leg weary from hard riding.

Coming to a halt Salar looked at the white gelding in the corral with some interest. It was too dark for him to see much so he could not tell the difference between the gelding and the Kid's big stallion.

"Is it the Kid's hoss?" Smith whispered.

"I think so. He would never leave that white devil of his with other horses," Salar replied, no more loudly.

"He's up at the house then," hissed Smith, swinging from his horse. "You stop here and watch the corral, Tonk, Sundon. The rest of us'll go up and look for him."

Four of the men started toward the house; the other two took up position to watch the corral. They drew and checked their guns; if the Ysabel Kid got by Smith and the other boys, they would be on hand to stop him when he came for his horse.

Smith and his party darted for the house; they did not draw their guns at first for there was nothing to be gained by charging into the building, gun in hand. Sanchez Riley might not be asleep and he was known to be a fast hand with a gun. He wouldn't take kindly to armed men charging about his place in the dark hours.

The men reached the wall of the dining room and moved along it. Salar halted by the window the Kid had looked through earlier, peering into the dining room. The lamp's light was fading as the oil in it burned away but there was enough to show the shape on the table.

"Is it the Kid?" Smith hissed, holding down the whisper to a pitch where it was only just audible.

"I'm nearly sure it is," Salar replied. "That looks like his hat and it was his horse in the corral. He'd sleep in here if he came after Riley was in bed.''

''I'll go in and down him,'' suggested the young gunman, still trying to redeem himself for his failure to take Dusty Fog.

''That'd be real smart,'' Smith answered sarcastically. ''We fire a shot and Sanchez'll be on us afore we can get out of it. We don't know who owns them horses in the corral, and they're not cowhosses. They might belong to a bunch of Rangers and we don't want to tie in with them.''

''You're right at that,'' Salar agreed, remembering that the Kid had many good friends who would investigate his disappearance. ''The less witnesses the safer it will be.''

''Sure,'' hissed Smith. ''You take Amp to the door there, Salar, and I'll go in the other with the button here. I'll sneak up and try to buffalo the Kid. If we get him like that we can tote him across the river and make it look like the Commanches got him.''

Salar did not care for the idea, but could not think of a better one so he moved into operation. Smith removed his boots and in stocking feet went through the door. At the other end of the room he could see Salar and the other man. The young gunman was behind Smith, gun out and cocked, his breathing sounding loud in Smith's ears.

Motioning the youngster to remain where he was, Smith moved forward. He lifted each foot with care and placed it down slowly, making sure there was no board to squeak a warning to the sleeping shape on the table. There was no move from the blanket-wrapped shape, other than the steady rise and fall as the Kid breathed.

Nearer moved Smith; his Dance Brothers' revolver heavy in his hand and his palm sticky. There was still no movement other than the Kid's steady breathing as Smith lifted his gun. Even with his hat over his head a hard blow from the barrel of the revolver should slow him down. Then they could all pile in, grab the dazed man and drag him outside.

The gun came smashing down with all Smith's strength. Then he gave a startled yell. The Kid was moving, rolling off the edge of the table. Smith's gun barrel smashed on the wood of the table top; his arm went numb with the force of the blow and the loading rammer burst from its retaining catch.

The Kid had wakened when the doors opened, laid waiting for the right moment, then moved. He took blankets and pillow with him as he rolled from the table away from Smith. As he fell the Kid threw the pillow at the lamp. His arm was good and the feeble light flickered out, throwing the room into complete darkness. He hit the floor and rolled under the table, gripping Smith's ankles and heaving. The gunman let out a wild yell as he was pulled from his feet, sprawling backward to crash into another table and knocking it over.

There was confusion among the other three members of Smith's party. They were in complete darkness and faced by a dangerous man who had the advantage of being able to shoot, or knife, any man he came across in the room, without the risk of injuring a friend.

Salai licked his lips and stood without moving; then lifted his gun from his waistband but did not cock it. The click would sound too loud in the silence. The Mexican was a night-fighter of some skill but did not care to take his chances in such circumstances. He hoped the others would have enough sense to remain motionless until the Kid betrayed himself, or until Sanchez Riley came with a light.

Slowly, silently, the Kid came to his feet. In the darkness his black clothing made him unseen. There was only one way out of the room, and that was through the window. It was not a pleasant thought. The window showed just a little lighter than the surrounding blackness so a man going through would make a good target for the guns.

Seconds ticked away slowly, then a sound reached the Kid, a low sound but one which told him all he wanted to know. Someone was moving towards him, sliding his feet along the floor, feeling carefully for any obstruction. The man could know little about night-fighting, or he would never have started moving so soon.

The young gunman moved forward, inching his way along the floor. He was sure his progress was undetected and meant to get close to the Kid. How he would know it was the Kid he never thought. This was his chance to make up for missing Dusty Fog in the Holbrock saloon. He cocked his Colt, the noise loud in the stillness. Vaguely he guessed there was someone near him and opened his mouth to whisper Smith's name.

A hand gripped the youngster's throat, clamping hard and stopping the involuntary yell which welled up. Then another hand gripped his shirt front and he was pushed backward, hard. With a violent heave from his unseen attacker he was reeling toward the window.

The Kid attacked in complete silence and with all his speed. He sent the youngster staggering toward the window then went sideways, flattening against the wall. He was only just in time.

The young gunman reeled, his shoulders crashing into the window. At the same moment there were three flashes of flame, two from the other end of the room; one from near at hand. The young gunman gave a single, shrill scream as the force of the bullets threw him backward. His shoulders went through the glass, wilted over and crashed out into the night. He was dead before he hit the ground.

The flashes of gun flame in the pitch blackness temporarily blinded the three remaining gunmen, but not the Ysabel Kid. He had known what to expect and his eyes were closed, missing the blinding effect when powder ignited and flared from the barrels of the guns. While the other men were blinded he was sliding along the wall, and opened the door just as Smith yelled:

"We got him, Salar! Light out!"

Salar and the other gunman turned to dash out and run for their horses. Smith saw the door open and thought that for once the youngster was acting correctly. There was no time to lose, already overhead were the sounds of men jumping out of their beds. The big gunman turned and left by the door, running toward the horses and not noticing that the youngster was not in front of him. He mounted and saw that one horse was still without a rider. He also saw whose it was and growled an angry curse.

"Roy," he yelled. "What the hell're you fooling at?"

"Where is he?" Salar snarled, watching the lights appear at the upper windows of the building over the dining room part they'd just left. "We've got to get away from here, and *pronto!*"

Then Salar guessed what had happened. It lent an urgency to their departure. The Mexican had been considerably surprised that the Ysabel Kid had made such an elementary mistake as to be skylined in the window. Now he knew that it was the young gunhand who lay dead outside the dining room window. There was a second, even more unpleasant point. The Kid was alive, unharmed and on the prod. At any minute his rifle or the old Dragoon might throw lead at them.

"Let's go," Salar hissed. "We didn't get the Kid."

The words brought instant departure. The other men knew of the skill of the Ysabel Kid and didn't want him in a fight. He had not returned for the white horse, but that meant nothing to them. They turned their horses and headed off into the night, drawing rein only when they'd put almost a mile between themselves and Sanchez Riley's place.

Salar brought his horse to a halt and the others stopped around him, straining their ears to pick up some sound which would warn that the Kid was in pursuit.

"We've lost him now," Smith growled.

"I ain't sorry, about that," put in another man. "That damned Kid's too much like an Injun for me."

"What we going to do about him?" Salar inquired. "Dave wants him dead and it'll go bad for some of us if he isn't. We can't get him before he crosses the river and I'm not going after him."

"We'll have to wait and see if he gets back."

"He'll get back, Señor Smith," Salar replied. "We might stay around here but it would do little good. There are so many ways the Kid could get back toward Holbrock without touching here. Besides, Sanchez Riley's the Kid's friend. He would be on the lookout for us."

"The Kid'll have to head back to Holbrock when he's done though," Smith remarked thoughtfully. "Which means he'll come through the woods, follow the trail. We could lay for him either in the woods, or where the trail comes out of them. That would be the best place, plenty of cover and less chance of the Kid getting hid down, with that damned yellow boy of his'n going."

"Is good thinking," agreed Salar. "One man could get on that rim beyond the woods and be able to see the Kid far off. Then we could lay for him. It will be the best way to get him."

"Mean sagehenning out there," Smith replied. "But it'll be worth it. We'll stay out and not let the folks at Holbrock know we're back. Then when the Kid comes through we'll be ready."

"He might come through in the night," the man called Tonk pointed out.

"Sure, but there'll be some moon in a few days and that white stallion'll show up real well."

With that Smith turned his horse and started in the direction they'd come. The other men followed him, riding away from Sanchez Riley's place.

The Ysabel Kid lay in the darkness away from the house for a time, listening to the sound of the departing men. Then he heard voices shouting from the opened windows of the bedrooms.

"What's the shooting, Frank?" called a voice as a man, keeping clear of the lamplight, came to the side of his bedroom window.

"I don't know, Jesse," came the reply. "You all right, Cole?"

"Sure, I'm all right," a third voice replied.

"Is all right, Señor James," Sanchez Riley's voice sounded from the ground floor. "A private matter. I apologize that your sleep was disturbed."

The Ysabel Kid was a day and a half into Comanche country. He'd crossed the Salt Fork of the Brazos before daylight on the morning after his visit to Sanchez Riley's and was now riding through the wild, open country of the greatest of the horse-Indians, the Comanche.

In that time he'd seen tracks of small hunting parties, not new enough to worry him, and sign of a large band but no warriors. He did not expect to see the Comanche until they wanted to be seen. He expected a Comanche scout had spotted him early that morning The scout would have seen him and gone haring off to warn others that a white man was in the land of the Comanche, or might still be watching to find out what folly brought a lone man into their land.

The Kid held his Nigger horse to the same easy walk; there was no need for hurry now and no chance of Salar's bunch following him. He studied the range around him, examining every inch for the first sign that the Comanche wanted him to be aware of their presence.

It was fine land here, rolling slopes, hills, valleys; rich and well watered. The grass was deep, fully capable of supporting and fattening vast herds of cattle. But the Comanche ruled this land and did not want cattle; only the great, shaggy buffalo, the mule-deer, the pronghorn antelope and the wild horse grazed on the rich grass. It was wild, beautiful, wide open and free from the corrupting influence of the white man. This was how all the plains must have looked before the white man came. Looking at it, the Kid felt a vague stirring, a half-wish that the white man had never come, bringing great herds of cattle and the rest: the town, the farmer, moving in and driving the free-roaming Indian from his land.

That would happen here, the Kid knew. The White Father in Washington might give his word that no white man would move across the Salt Fork of the Brazos, but that word would be broken. Pressure would be brought to bear on the Senate, more land would be needed, then it would happen again. The Army would move in and the Comanches would be driven from this fertile land to whatever useless bit of soil the white men did not want. That was the way of the white man; it was no wonder the Indians fought so savagely against it.

While he was thinking, the Kid was riding along, his every sense alert as he rode. He knew now he was being watched by cold eyes that followed his every move. But he made no attempt to draw either the Winchester or the old Dragoon revolver. He was here in peace and wanted to give no sign of war. Resistance would be out of the question and useless, for he was surrounded, watched, and the Comanche would show themselves only when they were ready, not before.

The big white horse snorted, throwing back its head as the wind brought the scent of hidden men.

"Easy, ole Nigger hoss," the Kid said gently. "I know they're about."

For another ten minutes he rode on, giving no sign that he knew the hidden watchers were around him, closing in all the time. It was the deadly war of nerves the Comanche liked to play on a man. One faltering move could bring an arrow or a bullet for the Comanche had no use for a coward or a man who spooked at shadows.

Then there were Comanches ahead of him. They came over the top of the rim he was climbing, to his right and left. Although the Kid never changed his easy position he knew there were others behind him.

The group were squat, thick-bodied, hard-faced warriors, with lank black hair framing their faces. They were naked to the waist, a breech-cloth and calf-high Comanche moccasins being all they wore. To men who didn't know the Indians in general and Comanche in particular, these warriors looked poorly dressed and armed. They did not wear fancy doeskin warshirts, feathered headdress or any of the war-wear affected by other tribes, nor did they show signs of either repeating rifle, war bow or revolver. Their sole weapon appeared to be the lance. Each man held the needle-pointed, razor-edged, seven-foot war lance, and wore a knife at his belt, but there was no sign of a firearm among them.

The Ysabel Kid was a man who *knew* Indians in general and more than a little about Comanches. The sign was plain enough and told a grim and savage story. Those warriors were Dog Soldiers, members of the bravest, finest, supreme Comanche war lodge. They carried the weapon of the chosen, the lance: it was the only weapon a Comanche Dog Soldier needed. His knife was not used to kill, but only as a means of taking a scalp, or ending the life of an enemy who did not deserve the honorable thrust of the lance. They used no bow, no rifles, no revolvers; but they'd be fighting long after lesser Comanches had been driven off and gone from the battle.

There was eight men in the group ahead of the Kid. Seven of them were old hands, battle-tired warriors with scalps hanging before their lodges. They sat their horses, faces expressionless and inscrutable, looking for all the world as if they were carved from stone.

The eighth Comanche was a youngster, just initiated to the Dog Soldier Lodge and without trophy or scalp taken in war. He watched the approaching rider, then lifted his lance, shook it in the air and let out a war yell which was savage enough to scare the hair out of a silvertip grizzly. He sent his wiry pony forward, changing from rock-still to a gallop in a split second and hurled down the slope at the Ysabel Kid.

The lance point, held along the neck of the racing pony, was ready to split through the Kid like a needle through a piece of cloth. The Kid stopped his horse for an instant, then started it forward again, still lounging in the saddle. For all his nonchalant appearance he was tense and ready and felt the big white horse moving more lightly now. Old Nigger always knew what was expected of him. The Kid kept on riding, making no attempt to draw a weapon but watching the young Comanche all the time.

At last, with the lance point driving full at him, the Kid moved. His right hand slapped down, knocking the lance to one side; his knee gave the white a signal. The big horse side-stepped the charging pony, allowing it to shoot by. The young brave was off balance and he did not get a chance to recover. The Kid lashed up a backhand slap full into the face of the onrushing Comanche, knocking him from the racing war-pony. As the young brave fell, the Ysabel Kid came out of the saddle of his big white. The Comanche lit down hard, lost his lance and lay winded on the ground. The Kid landed astride the brave, then knelt over him, the sun glinting on the blade of his razor-sharp bowie knife as it came out of the sheath to the brave's chin, resting in position to slit the brown throat.

"You live or you die," said the Kid in the deep-throated Comanche tongue, looking down into the brave's amazed eyes. "Choose!"

The young brave looked up taking in the dark face above him and reading no sign of hesitation. A refusal would bring the knife slashing across his throat, biting through to the neck bone. That was the Comanche way; the way of a Dog Soldier who took a prisoner in such a manner. The young Comanche hated having to choose life at the hands of a white man, no matter how well the white man spoke the Comanche language and knew their customs. Then he remembered. There was no disgrace in falling to the hands of this dark-faced Texan who rode the huge white stallion.

"I live!" he said.

The Kid came to his feet, stepping clear and sheathing the knife. From all around came the shattering yells of the Comanche braves and the thunder of hooves. They came down toward the Kid, riding with that superb skill which made them the supreme horse-Indians. It made an awe-inspiring sight: racing ponies, each ridden by a savage-faced warrior, armed and painted for war.

Suddenly, when it seemed that all the horses would collide and crush the Kid under their weight, they stopped as if some giant hand held them, halting their horses and sitting like statues again. The dust churned up by the hooves of the horses settled again and the circle broke to allow a grey-haired man to ride through. He came forward, face inscrutable, his eyes on the black-dressed young Texan. Sitting his huge horse the Indian looked at the Kid, not speaking.

Slowly the Kid lifted his right hand in a peace sign. The Comanche dialect rolled from his tongue again:

"Greetings, Long Walker. I have ridden many miles to see you."

"He's coming!" Salar yelled, bringing his horse to a halt by Smith's side. "I saw him in the distance."

"No mistake is there?" Smith replied.

It was the day the Kid was due back, nine in the morning, and the men were tired of waiting. They'd been camped out in the thick brush on the Holbrock side of the dense woods for the past few days, since losing the

Kid at Sanchez Riley's place. It was no fun for they were short on rations and could not get any more from town. They did not dare risk going into Holbrock for food for Dusty Fog was no fool and would guess what they were doing. Handling the Ysabel Kid was dangerous enough, without the added hazard of Dusty Fog and the sheriff.

"There's no mistake," Salar replied. "I didn't wait, but came as soon as I was sure it was the Kid."

Smith grunted. There'd been several false alarms over the last two days and nights. They'd turned out once in the darkness when a rider on a light-colored horse approached, only to discover they'd made a mistake. Now they were all bad tempered and irritable, wanting this business over and done with.

"Get hid out, then," Smith snapped. "Both sides of the trail."

They knew where to go for they'd already picked out the best spots for their ambush. Smith and two of the men took cover among the rocks at the side of the trail where they'd been camped, while Salar and the other men darted across the trail and flattened down among the bushes and trees at the other side. Salar slid behind a rock, his Buffalo Sharps in his hands, a bandolier, with the long .45 rifle bullets shining dully in the loops, around his shoulders. It was a weapon he favored above any other and could guarantee to hit a man-size target at half a mile. The range would be much less here. He set the adjustable rearsight, then looked around. He lay at the edge of a shallow gully, hardly more than the dried out bed of a long-departed stream. The edge of the water course and the bottom were lined with bushes and the streambed ran back to the wood.

The men lay in the places they'd picked, rifles ready, lining on the trail as it emerged from the woods. Because of their failure to catch up with the Kid, the men had come to regard him as almost a supernatural being. The feeling was playing on their nerves when they heard the faint sound of a man singing: a pleasant, untrained tenor voice.

"A Yankee rode into ole Texas,
A mean kind of cuss and real sly,
Who fell in love with Rosemary-Jo,
Then turned and told her, 'Goodbye.' "

Smith looked across the trail to where Salar was lying ready. The Mexican could read the angry, unasked question and nodded: he'd heard the Ysabel Kid sing before and knew the voice. The Kid must be thinking there was no danger so close to Holbrock, that he'd thrown off the pursuers and was safe. He certainly did not sound to be worried as he rode through the woods singing on:

"So Rosemary-Jo telled her tough pappy,
Who yelled, 'Why hombre, that's bad.
In tears you left my Rosemary-Jo,
No Yankee can make my gal sad.' "

Sweat was pouring down Smith's face; ever since the young gunhand was killed at Riley's there'd been doubt in his mind. He knew he was lucky to be alive, the Kid could easily have used his bowie knife when he dragged Smith down. There'd been no noise when the Kid moved in the darkness. Just that silent rush which sent the young gunhand sprawling backward into the window to his death. Not one of the men knew how the Kid got out of the room, or if he'd stayed in until they left. It was almost uncanny that a white man could move in such silence.

The song was going on, an old range ballad the men had heard many times before. They could imagine the black-dressed rider coming through the woods; he would be unprepared for the ambush and they'd have no trouble in bringing him down.

•   •   •

"So he whipped out his ole hawglegs,
At which he warn't never slow,
When the Yankee done saw him a-coming,
He knowed it was time for to go.
So he jumped on his fast running speed hoss,
And fogged it like hell to the West,
Then Rosemary-Jo got her a fortune
The Yankee knowed he loved her best."

The voice was coming nearer now, the lilting song sounding over the beating hooves of his horse. The waiting men tensed, caressing the triggers of their rifles, hoping they'd hear the end of the song before they cut off the singer.

" 'No, no,' she cried in a minute,
'I love me a Texan so sweet,
So I'm headed down to ole Dallas town,
This bold Texas cowhand to meet.'
So the Yankee rode down to the border,
He met an old pal, Bandy Parr,
Who run with the carpetbaggers,
And a meeting they held in a bar.
So Rosemary-Jo got word to her pappy,
He straddled his strawberry roan,
And said, 'From that ornery critter,
I'll save Rosemary-Joe, she's my own.' "

"One more verse, that's about all, Kid," Smith hissed under his breath. "It sure is a pity; I never heard the song sung all the way through."

The sound of the song and the hooves were closer now. The men lined their rifles, sighting on the opening from the woods. They'd let the Kid into the open, then send a volley which would tear him from the saddle.

•   •   •

"Now the Yankee done went to Dallas,
Met the Texan out on the square,
His draw was too slow and as far as I know,
The Yankee's still laying out—''

The horse came into sight, traveling at a fast lope.
The song ended just an instant before the big white
appeared. Smith's sighting-eye, along the blued barrel
of his Henry rifle, took in an empty saddle. He let out a
startled curse and was about to come to his feet. The
Kid was not in his saddle, nor was there any sign of
him.

The Ysabel Kid was no man's fool. Nor was he exactly unused to handling such situations at this. He'd
returned to Riley's place after concluding his business
with Chief Long Walker and Riley had told him what he
knew; one man was dead, and the others had gone,
their tracks headed back in the direction they came. The
Kid guessed what might happen on his return journey to
Holbrock and this place was the most logical for the
ambush. It would be out in the open and not in the thick
woods the men would lay in wait, for Salar would want
to be in the open where he could get the best use from
his Buffalo Sharps.

So, with this in mind, the Ysabel Kid was very alert as
he came into sight of the woods for the first time. He'd
seen the watching man, even recognizing Salar, and
knew what was happening. This made him ready for
trouble as he came through the woods, but he knew how
to handle it. His singing was to lull the waiting men's
suspicions, making them believe they were going to get
him served up like a plate of hominy grits.

The Kid left the saddle just as the horse came out of
the woods. He lit down at the edge of the trail, his old
yellow boy in his hands, ready to make some real fast
war. A shrill whistle left his lips and the big white's even
lope changed to a racing gallop, carrying it through the

ambush area before the men could fire at it. Once clear, the horse swung to one side, into cover, and stood waiting for the Kid's next order.

Then the Kid erupted through the opening, racing for safety and the shelter of a pair of close-growing cottonwoods. One of the men yelled, let loose of his rifle with one hand and pointed to the black-dressed shape of the Kid. The Winchester flowed to the Kid's shoulder and he fired without breaking his stride. The man stopped pointing, his hand flopped to his side, his rifle from the other hand; then he crumpled and went down, a bullet between the eyes.

The other four gunmen brought up their weapons, swinging to the new line. The Kid hurled over a small bush and lit down rolling. The first shots missed him, although Salar's bullet had drafted his neck as he lit down. Smith made a mistake; in his eagerness to get at the Kid he rose and brought his rifle to his shoulder.

"Get down, Smith!" Salar screamed.

It was too late. The Kid's roll ended behind the desired shelter of the two cottonwoods. The rifle appeared for an instant, cracked once, then disappeared again. It was out a bare two seconds, but in that time Smith was dead, hit in the head with a flat-nosed Tyler Henry .44 bullet. He was dead before his body hit the ground. He'd achieved one thing before he died: he'd heard all but the last word of the Rosemary-Jo lament song.

Salar licked his lips. That was Smith and Amp down, leaving Tonk on the other side of the trail; but Tonk was not the most staunch of men. He would dog it, if things got any stiffer. The man with Salar was looking worried too; things were not going as he'd planned. The Kid was not dead and could only be dislodged with considerable risk. There was also a chance that the wind might carry the sound of shooting to the town. If that happened Dickson would be headed out to investigate.

"We got to get him, Salar," the gunman called,

showing his shoulder and jerking it back as the Kid's rifle cracked. The shirt was torn and a bloody furrow burned across the man's shoulder.

Salar's Buffalo Sharps bellowed back, kicking a four-inch splinter of wood from the tree behind which the Kid was hiding, but doing no damage. It was a very fair piece of shooting, for Salar did not take a careful aim.

"Keep him busy," Salar answered. "I'll try and get through the woods behind him."

Before the other man could either agree or object, Salar had rolled down into the bottom of the streambed and started to move along it. His idea was to keep out of the Kid's sight, effect a complete surprise and avoid getting killed. The Winchester 66, with its comparatively weak, 28-grain load, was not a long-range weapon, but Salar was still well within range for the Ysabel Kid to make a hit.

From behind him, he heard the crack as the gunman fired at the Kid. Then from the other side of the trail Tonk opened up a bombardment which would help hold the Kid down and might even drown any slight noise Salar made when moving through the woods. The Kid was not firing back. Unlike the gunmen, whose ammunition was paid for by Stewart, the Kid had to buy his own, and did not intend to waste any needlessly. He watched the two men who were firing at him, keeping an ear cocked for any unusual noises and waited. His attention held by the gunmen caused the Kid to miss Salar's departure. The Mexican was not shooting but the Kid expected that: a Sharps bullet was a costly thing and Salar would not waste any, even if someone else was paying the bill.

The Mexican rolled down into the streambed and moved along it. He tried his best to combine speed with invisibility and was relieved when he saw the woods closing in on him. Carefully he climbed out of the streambed and faded into the woods. He paused to get his bearings, then headed on silent feet toward the trail.

At the edge he paused and made sure the Kid could not
see him before darting across to the shelter of the other
side. Then he stopped, sinking to the ground and lying
still. There was something wrong, he could almost feel
it. He remained still, listening, but could hear nothing.
The woods were as silent as a grave; the only sound was
the crackling of the rifles down trail. Yet Salar could not
throw off the feeling that things were not as they should
be.

At last he rose and moved on, but went with some
caution for he was dealing with a dangerous man. Salar
knew how keen the Ysabel Kid's senses were; a slight
noise would warn him. Then he would move and fade
into the woods like a shadow. Salar was good in the
woods, but he was not willing to match skill with the
black-dressed *gringo* devil.

Salar moved on, testing each piece of ground before
setting a foot on it and moving the other. He held his
rifle ready for use but it was an awkward weapon in a
fast-moving fight, especially in thick cover like this.

Suddenly Salar halted, his right foot poised in the air.
He lowered the foot with infinite care. Here was luck,
such luck as he never expected. It was only by sheer
chance that Salar saw what he did: another second and
he would have moved by. Through a narrow gap between the twisting undergrowth and tree trunks, Salar
could see the Ysabel Kid behind the two cottonwoods.
It was blind chance that he could see through to the edge
of the woods. The gap was narrow, but it would give
Salar the chance he wanted. There might even be thin
branches in the way, but that would make no difference
for Salar's Buffalo Sharps rifle. The .45 caliber 550-
grain bullet, powered by the explosive force of one hundred and twenty grains of powder, built up an energy of
around 2,300 pounds per square foot and left the barrel
at something like 1,400 feet per second. It would tear
through the thin branches in its path as if they were not
there at all, going straight into the Kid's back, killing

him before he knew what had hit him.

So Salar rested his rifle on the side of a tree, taking a firm grip on it and laying his sights with all the care he could manage. The picture was perfect, Salar's fingers caressed the trigger, starting to make the squeeze which would loose the bullet. He would accomplish what several men before him had tried unsuccessfully to do; he would kill the Ysabel Kid.

Then Salar relaxed slightly. A chance breeze moved a tree branch and partially obscured the Kid from view. Salar held his fire, the branch was thick enough to deflect the bullet: it might only be a slight deflection, but would cause the bullet to miss. If the bullet did miss, Salar knew where he would be: tangled in the Ysabel Kid's kind of country with a long, heavy and awkward rifle, a single shot rifle at that, against the Kid's handier Winchester. The instant that bullet missed, the Kid would be moving. He'd be back into the woods, hunting for the man who had fired. That Salar did not want.

That branch moved and Salar laid his sights again. This was the moment, the Mexican's breathing halted as he sighted. Then he stiffened up. The rifle barrel tilted into the air and slid through his fingers. He clutched spasmodically at the tree and slid down. The hilt of a knife rose from the center of his back.

A brown hand reached forward, gripped the knife and plucked it out. A second hand lifted the rifle, stripped the bandolier from the dead man's shoulders and moved them away. Then the hand took the Mexican's sombrero and threw it to one side and gripped the lank black hair. The wailing howl of a buffalo wolf rang out and the knife ripped around, biting into the flesh of Salar's forehead.

The Ysabel Kid's eyes flickered at the two gunmen. He glanced up at the sun and estimated the time. They would need displacing fast if he were to make it back to town. He knew he must deal with them now for he could not have them hanging on his tail much longer. They would have an easy target with the Kid riding along the trail in open country. He missed Salar down there: the man wasn't doing much at all. Yet the Kid did not know the danger he was in.

The wailing call of a buffalo wolf came to the Kid's ears. He turned his head to look back at the woods, then gave his attention to the men down the slope. Even as he watched, there sounded the flat bark of a rifle from the edge of the woods and the man who'd been with Salar jerked upright, staggered and went down once more.

Tonk saw the other man go down and stared for a moment, trying to see some sign of the Mexican. Panic hit him: Salar wasn't anywhere. He'd taken a Mexican stand-off, lit out when the going got dangerous. That was all Tonk wanted to know; he wasn't facing the Ysabel Kid alone. Turning, he backed away, then leapt to his feet and started running for the horses.

The Ysabel Kid saw what was happening; his rifle followed the man, lining on him, then spat once. Tonk felt as if someone had run a red-hot iron through his thigh. He gave a yell of pain and staggered, hit into a tree and tried to force himself on.

"Hold it!" yelled the Kid plunging forward from behind his tree and bringing up the rifle.

Tonk saw the black-dressed young Texan, saw the raised rifle and knew he was done. The range was such that the Ysabel Kid could hardly miss, or wound, again. If Tonk did not yell 'calf rope' fast he would get a bullet.

"Don't shoot, Kid!" he screamed back, holding on to the tree for support. "I'm done, don't shoot me."

Then Tonk's eyes bulged as he saw the dark shapes at the edge of the woods behind the Kid. He tried to yell a warning but the words would not come, so he raised a shaking finger and mouthed out vague, gurgling sounds.

"That's all right," the Kid replied, not turning to

look behind. "I know all about them. Me'n you's going to make us some talk."

"They'll kill us, Kid!" Tonk wailed. "I'm hurt bad—"

"Sure you are," answered the Kid without sympathy. "Bind your bandana around that leg; do it tight. Toss your gun this ways while you're about it." He paused and watched his orders carried out, whistling a loud note which started his horse back toward him. Then he looked down at Tonk. "Who killed that Chass hombre?"

"I don't know what you mean," Tonk replied, biting down his pain.

"Don't, huh?" grunted the Kid. He kicked Tonk's weapons well away, then turned to walk to his horse, gripping the saddlehorn. "Waal, *adios*."

"Kid. You can't leave me!" screamed Tonk, eyes on those grim shapes at the edge of the woods. "Kid, don't leave me here. You can't!"

"You wouldn't want to be betting on that, now, would you?"

"I'll talk, Kid. I'll tell you everything. Don't let them get at me."

The Kid turned and walked back. Tonk babbled out the full story of how Dexter Chass died, talking fast, eagerly, spilling all he could to the interested Kid. When the story came to an end the Kid grunted his satisfaction, then asked where the man's horse was.

"Over the rim. Don't leave me, Kid. They'll kill me."

"They won't," replied the Kid, grinning savagely. "You're born to stretch a hanging rope."

Tonk stared in terror as the Kid rode over the rim, then returned with a horse. The leg wound hurt badly but Tonk managed to mount his horse. He had to, for the Kid made no attempt to help him. In the saddle he gripped the horn with both hands, waiting for orders.

"Me'n you, friend," drawled the Kid, "we're going into town by the back way. You're going to take me to the sheriff's pound. Don't try nothing funny. Then you're going to tell the sheriff all you told me. Happen you don't, me'n you're coming out here again. I'll be safe enough – don't know if you will."

There was a three-handed game of poker going on in the sheriff's office. The players, Dusty Fog, Sheriff Dickson and Mort Lewis, were engrossed in their game and looked up with some annoyance as a man looked in through the door, and peered around at them.

"Folks're gathering down at the Long Glass, Jerome," he said. "Reckon it's about time you was getting the prisoner down there."

"What prisoner?" Dickson replied. "It's an enquiry that was started a week back. We'll bring the Kid down when he gets back and we can start."

"I'll tell them," the man answered. Looking pleased to be the bearer of bad tidings, he went on. "Dave Stewart's come back, got Scanlan and four more men with him. He's been to see Humboldt about starting the trial and I reckon he's going to get his way."

"All right, Tom," Dickson drawled easily. "Go back and tell them we'll be along at twelve o'clock and not before."

The man closed the door and left the sheriff looking at his fellow players. He met Dusty's eyes and they looked at the wall clock. It was quarter to eleven.

In the week he'd been waiting for the Kid's return Dusty had learned much about the town of Holbrock. He'd seen Stewart taking the two battered gunmen out of town, heading for his ranch. The rancher had not made another appearance in town until his arrival this morning. He'd come in alone but Scanlan and the other men could quite easily have returned to town without being noticed.

Dusty's stay gave him a chance to learn something about the people of the town. He'd spent some time with Humboldt, talking about the proposition which had brought him to the town. Dusty was satisfied the proposition would pay off for his Uncle but was not satisfied with Humboldt. The man was a shrewd businessman, but he was also an arrant snob. It took Dusty only one visit to the man's home to know this. He'd also learned about Humboldt's dislike for Mort Lewis. The townsman hinted regularly that he didn't think the Kid should have taken the risk of going to the Comanche country, but Dusty knew the concern was mostly to make a good impression on him.

"Reckon Humboldt might try and make you start the hearing early?" he asked.

"I don't know. Humboldt's being pushed to get the money for this notion of his. I reckon he might try to please Dave Stewart, not knowing how you feel about it, Dusty," Dickson replied, for he knew of Dusty's reason for being in town. "That's unless you've given him something definite to go on."

"Which I haven't yet," Dusty answered. "I wanted—"

Whatever Dusty wanted was never said. The rear door of the room was opening. Dusty came to his feet; hands crossing and the matched guns coming from his holsters, his chair flying backward. At the same moment Dickson flung himself sideways from his chair, hand fanning to the butt of his gun and Mort went over backward, throwing his chair and rolled toward the wall rack of weapons. None of them knew who was entering through the door, but were taking no chances.

"Sure didn't know I rated a civic reception," remarked a familiar voice.

The Ysabel Kid stepped into the room, a broad grin on his face, and pushing a limping, scared-looking man ahead of him.

"You damned crazy Comanche," Dusty growled, holstering his guns and eyeing his friend grimly. "I near on killed you."

"You near on done it afore," replied the Kid. "I tell

you, Dusty, it's like to scare a man bald, living round you.''

Dickson holstered his gun as he got to his feet and rubbed his hip which had hit the floor hard. His eyes went to the Kid, then to Tonk who staggered to the desk and sank into Dickson's empty chair.

"What happened to you?" asked the sheriff.

"He got his leg hurt a mite," the Kid answered for Tonk. Then he took the thin book from his belt, holding it out. "This here's what you want. And this *lobo's* got something he wants to tell you."

"No, I ain't!" Tonk yelled, then winced in pain as the Kid caught him by the arm and hauled him to his feet. "Where you taking me, Kid?"

"Back out'n town a piece," drawled the Kid, grinning meaner than the snarl of a buffalo wolf.

Tonk tried to struggle, but he was too weak from loss of blood and pain. On his face was a look of terror far beyond the pain he was suffering, a look the other men were hard put to explain. Dickson watched, frowning; he was not a man to allow needless cruelty, or the torturing of a prisoner. Then he remembered Tonk was one of the six who'd left town after the Kid; there were many questions which needed answering.

"I need a doctor, Jerome," Tonk whined. "I'm hurt bad."

"Sure," grunted the Kid unfeelingly. "That leg'll likely have to come off, happen it don't get seen to, and fast. But you aren't going no place until you tell the sheriff all you told me out there."

So Tonk talked, the words flooding out of him. What he said confirmed Dusty Fog's theory and threw a lot of light on the murder of Dexter Chass. Dickson looked at Mort Lewis for a long moment and opened his mouth to say something.

From the street came an ominous rumbling and tramping of feet. Dickson went to a window and looked out. Practically every man in town was coming along

the street. In the lead was Humboldt, Stewart and three
or four of the leading citizens of the town. Behind them,
at the forefront of the crowd, came Scanlan and Milton,
with two other hard-faced men.

"We could have trouble, Dusty," he warned.
"Stewart's been using his time to get them bunch all
stirred up."

Dusty went to the window. He'd handled crowds in
tough towns and knew the signs of a mob as well as did
Dickson. This was one coming, orderly yet, but a mob
for all of that. They were here to enforce their will on
Dickson and did not aim to be stopped by words this
time.

"Let's just you and me out first, Jerome. Learn what
they want. You and Mort stay on inside, Lon. Keep this
hombre quiet," Dusty snapped, then stepped up close
to Tonk, dropping his voice to a grim, urgent note.
"Mister, you need a doctor real fast. Just remember one
thing. The longer we are the less chance you've got of
keeping both legs. So when I call for you, come out and
tell the truth."

Dickson went to the cupboard and lifted Mort Lewis'
gunbelt out, passing it to the man, then he opened the
desk drawer and lifted out an Army Colt. "She's all
loaded and capped ready, Mort."

Quickly Lewis strapped on his gunbelt, settled it
down on his lean waist, then dropped the Colt into the
holster, making sure it was loose enough for a fast
draw. There was grim determination in his eyes as he
looked at the others. One thing Lewis was sure of, if it
came to shooting he'd something to settle with Scanlan.

"We don't want any shooting if we can help it,"
Dusty said, glancing at the neat handwriting in the diary
and reading what he wanted to know. "Remember, you
two stop in here until I give the sign. Bring this diary
with you when you come out, Lon."

With that, Dusty and Dickson went to the door.
Dusty drew it open and they stepped on to the sidewalk,

closing it again before any of the advancing crowd could see into the office.

The mob slowed down uncertainly as they saw the two men standing before them. Dusty was well enough known in the town to give pause to any man who meant to force trouble with the sheriff. But Stewart came on; his face held a vicious smile. Humboldt looked distinctly uncomfortable as he stepped forward with the rancher, while the rest of the leading citizens halted in confusion, allowing Scanlan and the other four men to move by them and fan out around their boss.

Humboldt stopped at the foot of the sidewalk, licked his lips and looked at Stewart who nodded in encouragement. The pompous-looking townsman coughed, then began to speak, his voice wavering and far from its usual booming note.

"Sheriff Dickson, as Holbrock's justice of the peace I demand you bring your prisoner, Mort Lewis, for trial."

"Right now?" Dickson gently enquired.

"Right now!" Humboldt agreed, and there was a rumble of agreement from the rest of the crowd.

"Before the Ysabel Kid gets back?"

"The Kid said seven days and he's not back yet," put in Stewart. "I don't reckon he'll be coming back again."

Dickson watched the crowd, they all appeared to have been drinking, maybe not much, but enough to make them willing to go along with a strong leader. All too well the sheriff knew how persuasive Stewart could be when he started talking. He could easily bring this crowd to believe they were being fooled by the law and that a plot to allow a murdering half-breed escape justice was afoot. Some in the crowd would believe it, others would go along just for the pleasure of raising hell.

"You said we'd hold off until noon today, when the Kid should be back," Dickson reminded them. "And

Mort doesn't come for the *hearing* until the Kid shows."

Stewart nudged Humboldt, causing the townsman to start nervously, and lick his lips. Then Humboldt gave a warning:

"Sheriff, the County Commissioners have held a meeting on your conduct and actions in this affair. We find them most unsatisfactory and are obliged to serve notice on you that unless you hand Lewis over for trial, we will be compelled to remove you from office and appoint a man who will do so."

"Just like that?" asked Dickson softly.

"That's right, Dickson, " agreed Stewart. "Just like that."

"Didn't know you were one of the County Commissioners, Dave," remarked Dickson. "You must have been elected real recent."

"You might say that. So how about it, Dickson. We may as well call off all this foolishness. The Ysabel Kid's dead."

The office door opened and a mocking voice said, "Lordy, they don't tell a body anything these days."

The Kid stepped through the door, leaving it open. He leaned his left shoulder against the jamb, the diary hanging in his left hand; his right hand hung negligently near the walnut grips of his old Dragoon gun.

Humboldt looked down and gulped as he saw the thin booklet. "Is that the diary, Kid?"

"Surely is, Judge."

"And you went to Long Walker's camp in the Comanche country to get it?" Stewart jeered, his disbelief plain.

"You reckon I didn't?"

Stewart's sneer grew broader, but the triumph was gone from his eyes. "You, one lone white man, went to the Comanche camp and brought it back with you?"

"Where else would I have got it from?"

"Could have been out at the breed's place."

"All right," drawled the Kid mildly, but there was nothing mild about the wolf-savage way his lips twisted in a grin. "What'd you want to show I'd been to Long Walker's village?" The grin was more twisted and savage then ever. "You mebbee want to see Long Walker his-self?"

"Yeah," sneered Stewart sarcastically. "We want to see old Long Walker."

The Kid threw back his head and from his throat came the wild, ringing imitation of a buffalo wolf's howl. From the rim which overlooked the town came an answering howl. There were startled yells as the crowd turned and saw that the rim was lined with Comanches, fifty or more of them, looking down at the town with cold, impassive eyes.

A grey-haired man rode his horse slightly ahead of the others, then halted without movement. Across his arm lay a Buffalo Sharps rifle which, even at that distance, Stewart recognized. The rancher licked his lips; that was Salar's rifle and he wouldn't have traded it off to the Comanche. That meant one thing and one thing only: Salar was dead and so were the other five men who had rode with him. On the whole, Stewart hoped they were dead, for it was trite but true to say dead men told no tales.

"That's Long Walker," an old-timer in the crowd shouted, pointing to the grey-haired Indian. "I saw him when he signed the treaty four years back."

"And like I said, I brought back that there diary," the Kid drawled. "It was in Mort's lodge, like he said it was."

"And it shows that Mort was at the Comanche camp on the eleventh," Dusty went on. "So he wasn't anyplace near where Chass was killed with the bullet from a combustible cartridge."

A cowhand in the crowd yelled, "Mort never used them sort. He used to laugh at us and say we couldn't handle a man-sized load, like he used."

"Don't listen to all this claptrap, Humboldt!"
Stewart bellowed. "If you and your bunch want me to
back that idea of your'n."

Humboldt gulped. He was in a real tight spot and
didn't know how to get out of it. Dusty had not given
him anything definite. He needed money urgently and
had listened to Stewart's offer to finance them. They'd
been warned that the trial of Mort Lewis was the condition for the money, so Humboldt had come along
with the demand for the trial to commence. Now there
was no need to try Mort and he could sue the town for
false arrest if they tried it.

"You're in a hell of a spot, Judge, aren't you?"
asked the Kid, mockingly.

"Yes, I am," Humboldt replied, speaking before he
realized what the Kid had said. His face turned redder
and he spluttered," I mean – er – that is—"

"Hold it, all of you!" Stewart yelled. "That don't
mean Lewis didn't kill old Dexter Chass. Harvey might
have been mistaken about how long Chass'd been dead.
Mort Lewis could've sneaked around to the Chass
cabin the day he come. . ."

"Chass wasn't killed in the cabin, Stewart," Dusty
interrupted. "He was killed when he found a bunch of
men pushing some of his stock on to the Lewis range."

"Yeah?" Stewart replied, hand falling to his side.
"Now who'd do a thing like that, and why?"

"To stir up trouble between Lewis and Chass is
why," drawled Dusty, watching the rancher all the time.
"As for who, the way I heard it, Tonk, Salar, Milton
and Scanlan."

The crowd caught the drift of the words and knew
what the next move was going to be. So, with one
accord they started to back off, one eye on the group
before the jail, the other searching for a safe place for
when Colt magic was made.

"Which of 'em shot Chass, if any?" Stewart asked.
"None of them. You did. Came up behind him and

shot from a distance. The bullet didn't go through, as it would have with the width of the cabin. Then you moved the cattle over the line, came back, picked up Chass and toted him to the cabin; left him face up on the floor. What you forgot was that the bleeding'd stopped and there was none on the floor. That told me what'd happened. Tonk confirmed it for me."

"Tonk?" grunted Stewart.

"Sure, the Kid got him alive, killed the rest of the bunch sent after him. He talked."

"Did, huh?" Stewart said. He knew Tonk would talk if captured. From what Dusty said, Tonk was a prisoner, and screaming loud enough to spill it all over the county. "Just fancy that."

Humboldt stood staring at the men, not knowing what to do or say. He was no fighting man and his reactions were far too slow for what was coming next. He stood as if fixed to the spot, his mouth hanging open as he realized that Stewart was accused of murdering the old man in the hills. It was all like a crazy nightmare, only far more dangerous than any nightmare could ever be.

Stewart grinned, a bitter, hate-filled grin. Then his hand lifted, fingers curling around the butt of his gun. At that moment the group before the jail broke into sudden movement.

Dusty Fog's hands crossed. Before any others, the matched guns were out, flame tearing from the barrels, throwing lead into Stewart before the man's Colt cleared leather. Even as Stewart spun around the rest were in action and gun thunder rocked the street of Holbrock.

Humboldt was trapped. His feet would not answer the terrified commands of his brain. He was in the line of fire and a serious hazard to Dusty's party. This could have been why the Yasabel Kid acted as he did, although Humboldt would always attribute it to the strength of his personality winning over a savage young man.

Whatever the cause, the Ysabel Kid moved fast. He flung himself forward, knocking Humboldt out of the way and bringing the fat, pompous man down in the street. Then, as they landed, the Kid rolled over Humboldt's well-padded body, hitting the dust of the street, and throwing lead into one of the two new Stewart men.

Milton was second off the mark in this whirlwind blur of action. His gun was flaming slightly before the sheriff's Army Colt threw down on him. Dickson felt the burning pain of a near miss as lead slashed across his ribs. His own aim was better; Milton rocked back on his heels, fell backward, sending one more wild shot from his twitching hands before he dropped the gun.

Scanlan's gun was out, lining on Dusty Fog when the door of the jail was thrown open and Mort Lewis hurled out with a Colt in his hand.

"Scanlan!" Mort roared, and his gun lashed flame sending a bullet into the big gunman's body.

Scanlan rocked under the impact of the lead, staggering and trying to shift his aim. Mort Lewis landed flat on the sidewalk, fanning the remaining five bullets up into Scanlan's body, shooting with savage speed and throwing him, limp as a rag doll, to the ground. Mort Lewis watched the man go down and his grim smile told that the death of his dog was avenged.

The last gunman lined on the rolling body of the Ysabel Kid, his first shot sending dust flying into the young Texan's face and blinding him. The Kid fired by sheer instinct, the heavy old Dragoon booming and sending lead into the man. The bullet struck an instant too late. Up on the rim, Long Walker saw the Kid's danger and showed that he was still tolerably fast for an elderly Comanche gentleman. The Buffalo Sharps came to his shoulder and bellowed out. The heavy bullet smashed into the center of the gunman's back, burying itself within inches of Humboldt's scared face. The gunman was thrown forward, full into the slamming power of the Ysabel Kid's Dragoon gun. He was dead before his body even hit the ground.

Then it was over. The thunder of shots died away and smoke drifted from the scene. Less than five seconds had elapsed since the first movement but Stewart was down, badly hit. Milton, Scanlan and the other two gunmen were dead. Dickson lifted a hand to his bloody side, knowing the wound was not serious or he would never have kept his feet to shoot back.

Slowly the crowd started to emerge from their cover; Humboldt came to his feet, face smudged with dirt and scared. He looked at the Kid who was standing up, rubbing the dust and grit from his eyes and cursing. This was the time for the leading citizen of the town to make a speech, praising the sheriff for an adroit job of work, but the words would not come.

Dickson looked at the crowd, cold contempt in his eyes. He stepped toward Humboldt, removing the badge from his shirt. "Here, you wanted this, now you've got it. Find another sheriff."

Humboldt stared as the star was thrust into his hand. "But . . . but . . . !"

The ex-sheriff didn't even look back, he turned to Lewis. "I know a town that wants a marshal and deputy Mort. Reckon we could take it on?"

"Reckon we could surely make a try," Lewis agreed. "Let's get your side fixed, then we can pick up my duffle and ride over to see."

Without even another word the two men entered the jail office and closed the door behind them. Humboldt watched them go, saw the impassive line of Comanches who were still watching the town and gulped down the words of apology he'd been ready to give, unwillingly, to Mort Lewis. Then he looked at Dusty Fog.

"Er . . . now this is all over, Captain," he began, the words rushing out, "I hope you and the Kid will be my guests until you leave. My daughter is coming home on tomorrow's stage. She's quite musical and I hear the

Kid sings well. We might have a pleasant musical evening.''

"Reckon it'd be all right?" inquired the Kid. "You didn't like having Mort Lewis around."

"That's different," snorted Humboldt. "He's a half-breed. I mean, you know about these people with Indian blood."

"Do we?" asked Dusty gently, without moving from the porch, his eyes flickering to the Ysabel Kid.

"That was why I suspected him from the start," Humboldt babbled on, not knowing what to make of this reaction. "It was wrong this time, but you know what these people with mixed blood are. He was part Indian and you can't trust a man with Indian blood, can you?"

There was a bitter smile on the Kid's face and a cold gleam in his eyes as he replied, his voice sardonic and unfriendly:

"Reckon you can't . . . say, how'd you like to meet my grandpappy?"

Humboldt was not a discerning man; he noticed nothing unusual in the way the Kid spoke. If it would put him in with Dusty Fog, Humboldt was willing to meet and entertain all the Ysabel Kid's kin.

"I'd admire to meet your grandfather," he boomed warmly. "But he doesn't live in Holbrock, does he?"

"Nope," replied the Kid, raising his hand in a salute to the old Comanche chief who was following his men off the rim. "He's up there, my mammy's father."

Humboldt stared at the dark, babyishly innocent, handsome face and the meaning of the words sank into his numbed brain. "You mean . . . you mean . . ."

"Sure," agreed the Ysabel Kid. "That was Grandpappy Long Walker up there on the rim."

PART II

The Quartet

THE WELLS FARGO stage coach might be the fastest form of public transport from Dodge City, through the Indian Nations, to Texas, but it was far from comfortable.

Betty Hardin reached that decision in the first couple of miles of the trip and now, within five miles of her destination at Bent's Ford in the Indian Nations, found no cause to change her mind. As she tried to find a more comfortable, or less uncomfortable, piece of the hard, stuffed-leather seat, she found herself hoping her cousin, Dusty Fog, would have better accommodation waiting for her when she reached the stage station at Bent's Ford. That was why Betty had come this way. Dusty Fog, Mark Counter and the Ysabel Kid had taken a herd to Mulrooney, Kansas, and were headed down trail again; she'd telegraphed, arranging to join up at Bent's Ford and would travel home to the Rio Hondo with them. She hoped they would have a horse for her, but even a buggy would be preferable to the hard seat of the coach.

She was a small, beautiful, shapely girl who would please the eyes of most men. Her hair was black, shining and long. Her face was tanned but not burned and harshened by the sun of her native Texas range. The skin was smooth and delicate looking and the features as near perfect as a woman could rightly expect. Her eyes were long-lashed and black and met a man's without distrust or promise. It was the face of a capable, self-controlled young woman who could become grimly determined when need arose. The hands of the OD Connected ranch would have sworn that the appearance did not lie, for Betty Hardin ruled the spread with an iron hand. Her figure was rich and full, the curves mature and eye-catching without being flaunting or provocative. The black bolero jacket and the frilly bosomed white silk shirt-waist emphasized her swelling breasts as they strained against the covering, but there was nothing of show about her. Her black divided skirt was long and concealed the trim hips and shapely legs without hiding them. On her feet were dainty, high-heeled, fancy-stitched boots with Kelly spurs strapped to them. Her hat, a snow-white Stetson, lay on the seat by her left hand.

All in all, Betty Hardin was a very attractive young woman, neither cold and aloof nor warmly inviting. She looked like an extraordinarily competent and capable young woman in what was still a man's land; asking no privilege, nor accepting any, because of her sex.

The three men traveling with her were an oddly assorted trio. They'd done little talking for the past day, having worked out all conversation early in the journey. Even the fat, loud check-suited whisky drummer no longer tried to impress Betty with his well-traveled intellect. He sat in his corner seat and puffed on his oily black cigar, blowing the smoke ostentatiously through the window. He'd tried to impress Betty with his talk of New York – until he found that she not only knew the city but was just returning from it.

Next to the drummer sat a soberly clad, stuffy-looking, prosperous businessman from an Indian Nations township. He didn't say much, tried to keep his expensive broadcloth suit from getting too dusty and failed. He'd refused, horrified, when offered a cigar and some whisky from the drummer's flask. His conversational efforts after that were restricted to an occasional groaned complaint at the discomfort of the coach.

The third man was a lean, mournful-looking, gaunt and poorly dressed Kansas nester who looked as if he carried the worries of the world on his shoulders. He was going to a Texas town where a kinsman had died and left him a small property. His main topic of conversation was limited to the poor farming of Kansas and how little money he'd managed to scrape together from selling his place.

Betty knew the man really did have little money; he ate only sparely and was obviously very close to the blanket. Though he was a nester and she born to the richest, largest ranch in Texas, Betty felt sorry for him and hoped he would have better luck with the property in the Lone Star State.

The girl moved again; she'd done much riding and not a little on the back of a horse which an Eastern lady would have thought half trained, but this hard stagecoach seat was worse than any saddle she had ever sat. Betty turned and looked out of the window at the brush- and shrub-lined route; they were following the winding line which the buffalo had made on their migrations across the plains. The stageline knew that the buffalo invariably picked the easiest and best-watered route, so they followed the tracks. The coach was approaching a bend and the birl braced herself against the lurching as it went around.

Suddenly, as the coach turned the corner, the driver gave a startled curse, hauled on his reins and kicked hard on the brake, bringing his team to a halt.

"Throw 'em high!" a voice yelled. "Reach for it, guard, or we'll cut you down."

There were five masked men standing in the trail, all holding Winchesters. The guard remained still, his shotgun across his knees. He left the weapon and raised his hands shoulder high, not offering to make a fight.

He was a guard, but not paid to commit suicide or endanger the lives of the passengers. That was Wells Fargo's orders; the guard must never risk getting a passenger killed. If there'd been fewer men he might have taken a chance, but a shotgun was a slow weapon and he would be cut down before he could shoot.

"Throw it down," the tallest of the outlaws barked. "And your belt guns."

The shotgun was tossed to one side, followed by the revolvers belonging to guard and driver. Then the tall man laid his rifle to one side of the trail and drew his revolver, ordering the two men on the box to climb down.

In the coach, Betty Hardin watched her fellow passengers. Her right hand rested just under the left side of her coat, but she remained seated. Her eyes went to the drummer; he was armed, wearing a Tranter revolver in a stiff holster which would effectively prevent a fast draw. Betty knew something of guns and gun handlers; she hoped the drummer would not try anything foolish in an attempt to impress her or save his wealth.

The other two men did not appear to be armed. The businessman looked flushed, angry and indignant at the outrage of being held up and robbed. The nester showed even more misery as the door of the coach was jerked open and the masked man looked in.

For an instant the outlaw seemed shaken to see a woman passenger. He ordered the men to climb out, stepping back to allow them to obey. Then he returned, holding out his hand to the girl.

"My apologies for disturbing you, ma'am," he said with exaggerated politeness. "I'd be obliged if you'd step out here with the others. Us honest road agents have to make a livng."

Betty stood up and accepted the man's hand as she climbed down. She saw the guard and driver were unarmed and altered her plans. She gave the five outlaws a glance which told her plenty, then joined the men who were standing in a line under the guns of the gang. The tallest of the outlaws advanced, keeping out of the line of fire and held out his hand to the drummer.

"Shell out, fatty," he ordered. "And don't try to pull that gun."

The drummer, face pale and his bluster gone, produced a thick wallet from his inside pocket. The outlaw accepted the wallet and tucked it into his waist band and went to the prosperous-looking man.

"Now you, senator," he said.

The businessman gave an angry snort, but produced a wallet. The young outlaw hefted it in his hand, flipped it open and shook his head.

"Sorry, senator. I can't see a rich gent like you traveling this light. You going to fork it over or do we take your pants with us when we go."

"This's an outrage," spluttered the businessman, but he reached under his shirt, fumbled and finally managed to pull out a thick, well-padded money belt. "I warn you, you ruffians. I'm a personal friend of Marshals Tilgham, Thomas and Madsen. They'll bring you to book."

"I bet they will, senator," laughed the outlaw stuffing the money belt through his belt and moving to the nester. "We wouldn't have took your pants, senator. Not with you having a lady along. Now, friend, how much you going to donate to this here deserving charity?"

The nester gulped, dipping his hand into his pocket and bringing out a thin chain purse. He held it out nervously, expecting to be beat over the head with a revolver for having so little wealth.

"This all you've got, friend?" the outlaw inquired, glancing into the purse at the five-dollar pieces. The nester nodded and the outlaw looked away. "Ben come here and search him. And watch how you do it."

Another of the masked men came forward, ran his hands over the nester's body then straightened and said,

"Cleaner than a hound's tooth, Jesse."

The outlaw called Jesse grunted. He stepped back and holstered his gun. Then took the drummer's wallet, opened it and extracted two ten-dollar bills, slipping them into the nester's purse before handing it back. Then he glanced at the driver and guard.

"What's in the box, boys?"

"Nothing, she's empty," the driver replied.

"No offense meant, but we'll just take a look," Jesse said. "Climb up and see, Ben."

The other man went behind and climbed up to the boot. He grunted in annoyance as he found it empty, then started to examine the luggage piled on top.

"Now, ma'am," Jesse spoke to Betty. "I'd surely admire a donation from you. Just give what you can spare, save enough to get you where you're going and let us boys have the rest."

"My bag's in the coach," Betty replied, a smile flickering on her face. "I'll get it if you want . . ."

"Jesse," Ben called from the top of the coach. "She's a Miss Hardin, and going to the OD Connected ranch in the Rio Hondo country of Texas."

Jesse looked at the girl; his brown eyes were all she could see over the mask which hid the rest of his features. "That makes you kin to Old Devil Hardin then, ma'am?"

Ben jamped down from the top of the coach as Betty nodded her agreement. "He's my grandfather," she said.

A gleam came to Jesse's eyes as he studied the girl. "'Reckon he'd pay well to get you back again."

"He might. But he'd be more likely to nail your hides to the corral fence." Betty sniffed, eyeing the man with contempt. "There's some money in my bag . . ."

"Not as much as Old Devil'd pay to get you back," Jesse replied. "Joe, keep a hoss out of that team and scatter the rest." He turned back to Betty. "I reckon you can ride, ma'am?"

"Do you reckon you could make me?" countered Betty.

Ben grinned, stepping toward her, his rifle in his right hand. The left lifted up Betty's chin, tilting her head back. "You're a spunky lil . . ."

The words ended, Betty moved fast, her fist swung hard, slamming into the young man's cheek and staggering him. He gave an angry snarl and was about to step forward when Jesse barked:

"Back off there, Ben! You asked for what you got. Our bunch don't mishandle no lady."

Two of the outlaws were unhitching the team from the coach, working with a speed which showed they knew their way around harness horses. All but one of the horses were sent galloping off in the direction the coach had come. The other horse was held by one of the gang ready to be used for the kidnapping.

"Now, ma'am," Jesse said to Betty. "Me'n my gang don't use no violence against a lady like you. So, iffen you won't get on that there hoss and ride with us I am going to cut down this bunch one after the next until you come."

Betty watched the young outlaw's eyes as he spoke. At different times, on the OD Connected, she'd met most of the top Texas gunfighting men. She'd seen the smoothly efficient killers like her cousin, Wes Hardin and Ben Thompson, King Fisher, Clay Allison or Mannen Clements. This boy was not in that magic class but he would do just what he said if she did not obey. From his appearance and the way he acted Betty knew he would not hesitate to shoot down an unarmed man to keep his word.

The guard caught Betty's eye and made a sign, but she almost imperceptibly shook her head. The man was willing to risk his life to try and save her but she did not want it. Any attempt would lead to bloodshed and none of the men from the stagecoach would be left alive. There was no need for such a risk, not with Bent's Ford

five miles away. By Betty's reckoning there should be
three men who, individually or collectively, could sing two
gangs like this to sleep one handed. Left handed at that.

So Betty agreed to go along and not raise any ruc-
tions. She watched them checking through the baggage
as Ben went up once more and pitched it down to them.
Jesse asked which of her belongings she wanted to take
with her, so she pointed to her over-night bag.

At the time Betty watched the young men, studying
them with eyes which knew the West and knew the
signs. They all wore cowhand-style clothes, but they
were not cowhands. Every one of the five wore ready-
made boots, which no cowhand worth his salt would
think of doing and their hats were cheap woolsey. The
gunbelts were another pointer. The tall leader, Jesse,
wore a good belt, but it did not hang as well as it might
and appeared to have been made for a more portly man.
The other four wore belts which showed signs of crude
alterations, small things like leather being cut away to
leave the trigger-guard clear of the revolver.

The signs told Betty she was tangled with a bunch of
youngsters full of the so-called excitement and adventure of being outlaws. The way they were acting showed
that they'd been reading the lurid fanciful stories which
were being written about such outlaws as Jesse and
Frank James. The politeness to her, the slipping of
money into the nester's purse instead of robbing him,
were all part of the pattern. The leader would use the
name Jesse to try and make people believe he was Jesse
James.

Betty smiled. In New York and on the trains she'd
seen books like *True and Factual Life of Jesse James*,
which showed the Clay County outlaw as an unselfish,
kind, noble Robin Hood using a Navy Colt instead of
yew longbow. The girl had never met the famous Dingus
James, but had heard Dusty Fog's views on him as both
a Confederate Army hero and a train and bank robber.
They were not complimentary, but more truthful to the

outlaw's real nature than the fanciful stories in print.

Her smile broadened as she remembered her cousin's reply when one of the younger OD Connected hands had spoken of Jesse James robbing only the rich. "Sure," was Dusty's reply. "Jesse wouldn't rob the poor. They'd have nothing worth taking."

Which summed up Jesse James's generous behavior.

These young outlaws were trying to copy the fictional Jesse James. Their behavior was proof of it, and there was more to come.

Jesse gave an order and one of the gang went to collect the horses, but they were not the fine, fiery steeds such as the James gang were supposed to ride when on their missions. The horses brought back looked to be the culls left behind in some trail-end town as not worth taking back to Texas with a trail driver's remuda. If horses like that had ever been found in the OD Connected remuda, even as culls, there would have been hell raised by Ole Devil.

"Joe," Jesse snapped, as he looked at the harness horse from the scattered team. "You take that hoss. We can't have no lady riding bare-backed with us. She can have your hoss."

Betty was grateful for the thought, although she almost wished to be riding the stage coach horse, it looked as if it could outrun those saddle horses given half a chance. She accepted the horse indicated by the outlaw called Joe and allowed Jesse to help her mount.

"How about them weapons down there?" Ben growled, jumping down from the coach and fastening Betty's bag to his saddle horn.

Jesse looked at the shotgun and the two revolvers which the guard and driver had dropped. "They belong to you boys?" he asked.

"Sure," the guard replied. "I bought the scatter a piece back and Wells Fargo don't supply revolvers to us no more."

"We'll leave 'em then," announced Jesse, magnanimously waving his hand. "My bunch don't take nothing from a man doing a job of jobs. If they'd belong to the Wells Fargo bunch we'd have taken them, but not from you. Don't try and touch 'em afore we're out of sight."

With this final gesture Jesse flipped the loop of his rope around the neck of Betty's horse, turned and rode off, the others following him. The girl accepted this more as a tribute to prowess as a horsewoman than for any other reason. It could hardly be due to the horse, it was a sorry creature, the worst of a bad bunch and would be unable to outrun any of the others.

Betty did not mean to try and escape. If she succeeded, the gang might go back and kill the men from the stagecoach. They would stop their polite treatment if she tried and failed. It was as well not to take any chances or give any provocation to a bunch like this. They were as dangerous to fool with as a fully loaded, cocked Colt revolver; safe to a certain point, then deadly.

The guard and driver watched the gang taking Betty away. Their thoughts ran on the same lines as Betty's, seeing the gang as the dangerous amateurs they were. Neither man liked letting the girl go without a fight and knew the sooner they made Bent's Ford the better it would be. They could not make it before dark, that was sure and no pursuit could be organized before the morning. The guard spat disgustedly, turned and walked to pick up his weapons.

"A fine thing!" yelled the businessman, staring after the fast-departing gang. "An armed guard and we still get robbed. I'm not without friends among the Wells Fargo superintendents, my man. I'll see this gets reported."

"You do that," grunted the guard, holstering his Colt and tucking the shotgun under his arm.

"Why didn't you do something?"

"Like what? That was a dangerous bunch there. Happen I'd tried to fight them off they'd killed the lot of us."

The businessman's face lost some of the indignation as he listened to the guard's words. He gulped and watched the guard and driver starting to walk in the direction of Bent's Ford.

"Jesse!" he gasped to the whisky drummer. "They called that outlaw Jesse. We were robbed by Jesse James."

The drummer did not reply. He'd drawn the same conclusion as the businessman and was not waiting around to discuss it. The only men who were armed had started to head for Bent's Ford and he did not aim to be left out here. Without a word to the other two passengers he started off. The business man and the nester exchanged looks then departed hurriedly in the tracks of the others.

The outlaw band and their prisoner rode overland from the stage trail. Once away from it, Jesse reached up and pulled off his bandanna, wiping the sweat from his face. He was a good-looking young man, but there was a weakness about his mouth which did not fit in with his pose as a masterful outlaw. He looked a young man who would not take kindly to hard work, and had probably lived on petty crime until getting ambitious and starting this gang.

"Shouldn't let the gal see your face, Jesse," the one called Ben growled.

"Have a hell of a job not to," grinned Jesse. "It'll take a piece afore we can get paid off for her and we can't keep the bandannas on all that time."

"She'll know all of us," objected the one riding the stageline horse.

"That's right, she will," agreed Jesse. "Do you bunch reckon that we're going to let Jesse James or Sam Bass get the credit for our job." He snorted angrily. "Like hell we are. Not even Jesse James ever pulled a stage hold-up and a kidnapping right after each other."

Betty hid her smiles, gripping the reins in her dainty, gloved hands and rode easily; Jesse must think there would be some special distinction in kidnapping Ole Devil's granddaughter. He was also afraid that some other famous outlaw would try to sneak his thunder. She wondered how he was going to get word over all those miles to the Rio Hondo to get the ransom money back.

So did Ben. He drew off his bandanna with a sigh of resignation, showing a sullen, mean face with a sprouting of downy whiskers on his jowls.

"How you fixing to let her kin know, Jesse?" he asked.

Joe, trying to get comfortable on the bare back of the stageline's horse, grinned. He was a moronic-looking youngster of perhaps seventeen, and looked enough like Jesse to be his brother. He was also proud of Jesse and regarded him as smarter than he was.

"Don't you just reckon ole Jesse got it all worked out?" he asked.

Jesse apparently had not got it worked out, but his brain was working on it. Betty decided to help out.

"You could send a letter to Bent's Ford," she suggested. "Find another stage that's headed there and send word to Bent. Tell him what you've done and suggest he telegraphs Grandpappy. Then, likely, Grandpappy will send back for him to pay you."

"Sure, that's just what I was going to say," said Jesse, looking relieved. "Bent's a Texas man and Ole Devil'll deal through him. Save us keeping you with us for too long, ma'am." He paused and thought out the rest of the idea. "We'll tell him to get the money, send up a smoke signal when it's ready and we'll let him know who to deliver it to us."

The idea showed careful thought. Betty made the suggestion in case something went wrong and the tracks left by the gang were wiped out so that the Ysabel Kid could not find them. This way the letter, delivered to a stagecoach, would give Dusty Fog and the others somewhere to start in the search.

It was not really likely that the message would ever be sent. At dawn Dusty, Mark and the Kid would be on her trail. The Kid could follow a line with the skill of his Comanche grandfather and would find the gang. Dusty could easily raise a plan which would liberate her from their clutches.

Betty was almost sorry for the young men. Jesse and the others were not really bad, just misguided. They'd chosen a life of outlawry believing it to be a gentlemanly and easy way of making a living. They were going to learn that it was not the best way of life for a man and was full of danger. She hoped they would learn from this lesson and not be shot down trying a robbery where the guard could handle his guns.

Despite Betty's thoughts to the contrary, Jesse was not without some of the basic outlaw skills. They pulled their horses up as they came level with a stretch of rough, rocky ground which made a contrast with the grassy range. Betty expected the outlaws to ride their horses on to the rocky ground to prevent them being followed. But Jesse did not; he brought the horse to a halt and stopped the others.

"Here y'are, Ben," he said, handing the other his reins. "Take off with the hosses. Make a big circle, then scatter them."

He removed the saddle from his horse, followed by Sim and Jube, the other two members of the gang. Sim was a pleasant-looking youngster, and Jube, chubby and cheerful, but a poor hand with horses. They stripped off their saddles, handed the reins to Ben and waited for Joe. The youngster was looking puzzled.

"Ain't but enough hosses for us four over there, Jesse," he said, pointing across the rocky land to a large outcrop of stones.

"We'll take that hoss you're on then," Jesse replied. "Ride it over there and see that everything's all right."

For a moment, while most of the gang were on foot, Betty was almost tempted to make a break for it. Then she held her hand. They obviously knew the country far better than she did. It would be dark before she could get back to the stage trail and make Bent's Ford. She could find her way back in the light but did not want to try it in the dark. Jesse might treat her gallantly but he would be nasty if she caused him any trouble.

The three men swung their saddles on to their shoulders and Jesse nodded to Betty to dismount. There was a delay while Joe off-saddled her horse, then she was requested to lead the saddleless horse which Joe had ridden. Taking the reins Betty followed the men, stopping to watch Ben riding off across the grassy land, leading the other horses and making a good, bold track. Jesse saw the girl watching and his chest puffed out with pride.

"I thought of that idea myself," he said proudly.

"Real smart," Betty answered.

"Sure. There'll be a posse after us, but they'll follow Ben and the hosses. He's smart, Ben is. Take them for a hell of a run, if you'll pardon the word, ma'am. Then turn the hosses loose and scatter them and swing back to our hideout. They'll never find us."

Betty did not reply to this, although she could have told Jesse what he had failed to think about. She followed the men across the hard ground, knowing how little sign they were leaving. Carefully she slipped off one of her gloves and let it fall to the ground, unseen by the men. It would be a marker for the Kid.

Four horses were hidden among the outcrop, but they were of no better quality than the four left behind. Betty snorted angrily for they must have been without water for some time, but Jesse wasn't cruel and he watered them before they rode on. Just before dark they reached a shallow, rocky-bottomed, fast-running stream. Jesse grinned at the girl as they rode into the water, then turned upstream. They followed the stream for a time and Betty slid off her second glove, tossing it into the branches of a scrub-oak as they scraped under it, the branches tugging at their legs and along the flanks of the horses.

Just before it was too dark to see, Jesse brought his gang on to the shore and led them on. Betty tried to get her bearings. She dropped her handkerchief soon after they left the stream but had nothing more to use for a marker. She doubted if it would be needed, for they had come from the rocky and barren ground on to grass which would hold a track.

The girl was used to long hours of riding and was pleased that her trip to the East had done little to soften her. The men did not mean to stop, that was for sure. They pushed on through the night and came onto a trail which led down through a small town. Betty watched the silent and deserted buildings knowing that people were sleeping inside. She felt a hand on her arm and turned to see Jesse by her side. The young man held his revolver, the barrel pointing at her side. She nodded, reassuring him that she did not mean to make any foolish outcry. They passed through the town and stuck to the trail for a time before turning onto a narrow, winding path which led through some rough, wooded country. The girl knew they'd been riding almost all the night and it would soon be dawn. She also knew that they were not far from the scene of the holdup. Her instinct for direction was working and told her they'd ridden in a wide circle.

A dark shape loomed up ahead of them. Jesse halted his gang, slid from his horse and advanced across the clearing toward a small farmhouse. A moment later he gave a whistle and the others rode toward him. He stood in front of the house and waved his hand.

"Climb down, ma'am," he said. "This here's where we hide out."

Betty climbed down; she felt stiff and sore but knew it would go off. She walked onto the porch as Jesse opened the door and stepped inside. She heard him fumbling around and then lighting a lamp. Stepping into the living room of the small two-room building, Betty looked around with distaste. The room was furnished with rickety old chairs, a table and a cooking stove. It was dirty, littered with food scraps, old newspapers and assorted junk.

"Reckon you'll feel a mite hungry after your ride, ma'am," Jesse said. "Set a spell while Joe here cooks up a meal."

The girl watched Joe light the stove and take up a filthy frying pan and a battered coffee pot. He set both on the stove and opened a cupboard to take out some eggs. There was other food there, ham, bread, butter and beans, but he left them alone.

"Ole Joe's not the best cook, but he licks the rest of us," Jube remarked, speaking directly to Betty for the first time and blushing furiously.

That was obvious to the girl. She watched Joe's clumsy way of handling the frying pan; then as he broke an egg into the half-ready fat she snorted. She hated to see things done badly when she could do them better. She crossed the room and pushed Joe to one side.

"Ugh!" she snapped, making a wry face as she looked at the blackened, burned mass of fat and the egg. "And am I supposed to eat this?"

"Why not?" Jesse grunted huffily. "We've been eating it."

"You're forgetting I'm a lady," Betty answered, hoping her Cousin Dusty would never hear she'd made the claim. "I bet Jesse James wouldn't serve food like this to a *lady* prisoner."

That was all Jesse needed to hear. He would not want Betty to say she'd received anything but the best treatment while held by his gang. There was, however, a problem – none of the gang could cook any better than Joe.

"All right," said Betty, "I'll cook for you. Heat me

some water and wash out the frying pan, Joe. Get it clean. Jube, you can clean these plates and cups," she indicated a pile of dirty, unwashed crockery on the table. "Sim, see if you can find a broom and clean this place out. No good expecting a lady to put up with this for an indefinite time."

Jesse scowled, but gave the orders and the others went to work. Betty watched them, almost forgetting she was a prisoner as she prodded them with a biting tongue. She knew how to handle young men from her experience at the OD Connected. By the time Ben arrived the place was much cleaner and Betty was about to start cooking the meal. None of the outlaws gave any thought to her wearing her short jacket even while cooking. They were licking their lips at the aroma of decently cooked food. But they were not going to be left in peace for their meal.

"I won't sit at a table with you bunch dripping trail dust all over it," she stated firmly. "Wash up and make yourselves look respectable."

There was some grumbling, but the food looked good and they obeyed Betty. There were long faces and the five were beginning to wish they'd never thought of kidnapping a determined young lady like Miss Betty Hardin.

It was near daylight when the meal was finished. The gang tired from their long day and night in the saddle, wanted to get to sleep but Betty insisted that everything be tidied up again, the cups and plates washed and the food cleared away. There was grumbling, especially from Ben, but Jesse insisted that they maintain their pose as gentlemen outlaws.

"How about sleeping, ma'am?" Jesse asked when everything was done to her satisfaction. "Ain't but the one bed in the next room. You can have it and we'll lock you inside."

Betty did not argue. She knew just how far she could risk pushing the young outlaw and there was a chance she could escape while the men were asleep. The idea was dispelled as soon as she entered the bedroom. There was only the one door, and the window was boarded up firmly. She could see no chance of breaking through the boards without a whole lot of noise. Betty did not even mean to try. Already the search for her would be starting and, with luck, nightfall should see her safe in the company of her friends.

So Betty lay on the bed. There was a knock and the door opened. Her right hand slid under her coat toward her left armpit and stayed there as Jesse came in, carrying several blankets.

"Hope you'll be comfortable, ma'am," he said politely, and laid the blankets on the end of the bed. "We'll send off that letter as soon as the boys have got some sleep in."

"Why thank you, sir," Betty replied. "It's surely pleasant to be caught by a gentlemanly bunch of owlhoots like you."

Jesse was almost bursting with pride as he left the room. Betty heard the lock click and lay back smiling. There was no danger, so she went to sleep.

A knocking on the door woke Betty. It took her a few seconds to think where she was. Then awareness flickered and she sat up, carefully straightening her coat, particularly the left side of it. She swung down from the bed, rubbing her eyes and stretching to relieve the stiffness caused by sleeping after hours of riding.

The door opened and Jesse called: "Can I come in, ma'am?"

"Come ahead," replied Betty.

"The boys was wondering if you'd do them the favor of cooking up another meal, ma'am," Jesse said as he entered.

"Why sure," Betty replied. "What time is it?"

"Near to four in the afternoon, ma'am."

"Well, tell them to peel some potatoes ready for me," ordered Betty, and made another stipulation which did not meet with approval when it was passed on.

"I'll be damned if I'll do it!" Ben bellowed.

But he did. The smell of the meal brought about a change in Ben's attitude. He grumbled about it, swearing he'd never get involved with kidnapping another woman. Then he joined the others and for the first time in his life had a second wash in a day. Worse, he was forced to shave off the stubble he proudly called a beard.

"Looky here, Jesse," he growled when the meal was over. "Let's get this letter sent off and shift this gal back to her kinfolk."

"Yeah," agreed Sim. "I'm thinking we done the wrong thing in bringing her here to our hideout. I'm for going into town and catching the stage that goes through to Bent's Ford. Sooner they get to know where the gal is and how much we want for her the happier I'll feel."

Jesse was beginning to think the same thing. He used the inside of a coffee packet for his letter, writing with the stub of a pencil. The gist of the letter was that he was holding Betty Hardin for ransom and wanted ten thousand dollars for her release. He explained the arrangements he'd thought out the previous day and did not sign the letter. He was proud of the note and wished he could show it to Jesse James, Sam Bass and the other great outlaws.

"I'll take it, Jesse," Ben said with surprising eagerness, for he was never one to go in for doing any kind of work. "I'll get me some supplies in town, now we all got our share of the loot."

"Reckon I'll come with you, Ben," Sim put in quickly. "Feel like taking a ride."

"I'll come in as well," Jube spoke up. He was shy around any female company and sidled past Betty as if he thought she was going to explode any minute. "I reckon you 'n' Joe can handle things here, Jesse."

Jesse did not like the idea, but could see there was

mutiny in the air. He was wise enough not to push his gang too hard. He and his brother could take care of Betty and the other three would not get into any trouble in town.

Ben, Sim and Jube mounted their horses, the bay, the washy sorrel and the roan. Then Ben noticed Betty's overnight bag was still fastened to his saddle horn. He was about to throw it on to the porch but snorted, fingering his smooth cheeks. The hell with her, let her do without it for a spell. He stuffed the small bag firmly between the cantle and his bedroll, then sent his horse running for town.

Betty spent the rest of the afternoon and early evening listening to Jesse's stories of the holdups he'd done and the ones he planned to do. She felt sorry for him; he was so sure he was the greatest outlaw the West had ever known and she guessed he would very soon get dissuaded in his belief.

Night came and the lamp was lit. They sat around the table, playing poker with a greasy old deck of cards Joe produced. Time was passing and there was no sign of the other three outlaws.

Jesse lowered his cards, listening intently; then he came to his feet. The others could hear the sound of horses approaching and Betty's eyes gleamed. Jesse looked worried; he rose and went to the window, looking out into the night. When he turned there was a hint of panic in his eyes that worried Betty.

"What's wrong, Jesse?" asked Joe, also standing.

"I don't know. If it's the boys they haven't given the whistle."

Betty thrust back her chair and came to her feet. Even as she did so she knew she'd done the wrong thing. Jesse leaped forward, gripping her arm and turning her. He threw his left hand around her shoulders, dragging her to his body. There was a low click as he flipped open the knife he pulled from his pocket and held the sharp blade near her cheek.

"Keep your mouth shut!" he hissed, and there was fear in his voice. "See who it is, Joe!"

Joe went toward the door and from outside came the sound of singing. Drink-loaded, whisky-primed, drunken singing.

Bent's Ford was something of a mystery to strangers seeing it for the first time. True, there was a lake of clear blue water near the three buildings which formed the metropolis, stage relay point, cattle watering stop, saloon, dancehall and gambling house. Yet nowhere was there anything which needed fording: the only stream was barely wide enough for a Texas longhorn to wade.

The name came about from the cowhands' sense of humor. A Texas trail hand in Abilene was being pestered and questioned by a dude in search of knowledge. On being asked how they moved cattle over a river he told of Bent's Ford, on the mighty Bent River in the Indian Nations. The story got around and grew until now there were dudes who believed that Bent's Ford was the only crossing of a river so deep that three stern-wheelers sunk bow down, one on top of the other, couldn't be reached with a hundred-foot sounding cord. The river was so wide that it could barely be seen across, except on a very clear day, and in it were brook trout as big, fierce and dangerous as Everglade alligators. They were so ravenous that a man trying to swim the Bent River was likely to be pulled under and eaten alive. These and other stories were built on the narrow stream and Bent's triple business of stage station agent, saloon keeper and store owner became known along the length of the cattle trails as Bent's Ford.

Duke Bent did not protest at the legends and windies about his place. He'd even helped to build a few of them himself, for they were good for business. The Wells Fargo Company found it a useful place for a relay station. The trail drives came to the lake for the purpose of watering their cattle. The trail boss could buy fresh supplies in Bent's store and spend a pleasant evening in the saloon, dancing with Bent's hostesses or gambling at one of the games. Here it was fair gambling: the stakes at the poker games often ran sky high but there was never a hint of crooked play. Duke Bent began his life on a Mississippi stern-wheeler and knew almost all there was to know about the detection of crooked gamblers. Once detected, he could handle trouble any way it came, for he was a big, powerful man and fast with a gun.

All in all, Duke Bent should have been contented with life. He was rich, liked and respected, his business flourished, unhindered by the Indians, who were moved by the bountiful United States Government into Oklahoma Territory. There was no trouble in the air; the last drive had gone up trail the day before and the next was not due until the following week. He should have been happy to relax, taking trade from the men drifting down to Texas from earlier drives, the occasional farmer moving through the territory, and the stagecoaches. The fact that the expected stage was not here, and it was already dark, did not worry him; stagecoaches were often delayed and late.

His discontent was explained to the two men who stood at the bar in the saloon section of his business.

"There ain't one in the house," he groaned, and the other two looked disappointed.

It was a tragedy of the first water for Bent. He cared little for wine, was married and found his attention to women seriously curtailed, so his other, and most prevailing interest – song – was all that was left. Bent had been very happy when the Ysabel Kid had rode in that afternoon, for Marshal Chris Madsen was on hand. Here was Bent with two really good tenors, all set to throw in his powerful rolling bass to some quartet harmony and there was no baritone. It was a real tragedy. What good was a session of quartet singing without a baritone.

Bent was not a man to accept defeat. He'd been around the customers without success; there was not a baritone in the house. Now he came back to the bar looking miserable.

U.S. Marshal Chris Madsen, a tall, lithe young man, leaned his shoulders against the bar. He wore range clothes and around his waist was a gunbelt which supported an ivory-handled Cavalry Colt Peacemaker. His face was pleasant, his hair brown, and his moustache neatly trimmed. He was one of Oklahoma's "Three Guardsmen" and along with Marshals Billy Tillghman and Heck Thomas was trying to rid the Indian Nations of outlaws.

"Sure is hard luck, Duke," he agreed, then turned to the lean, black-dressed, Indian-dark young man by his side. "Where's Dusty and Mark, Lon? Ole Mark'd do for the baritone part, seeing as how we can't get a better one."

"They'll be along in a couple of days," replied the Kid, looking a little sheepish at the question. "They stayed on in Mulrooney."

The truth of the matter, and the Kid did not care to tell the others, was that he'd deserted his two friends. He'd left behind the two men who were closer to him than brothers to face an ordeal, and run out like a scared jackrabbit. He'd not felt like singing at all, but Bent expected it and would ask too many questions if the Kid did not join in. He sighed, hoping Dusty Fog and Mark Counter would come through the ordeal he'd left them to. He should have stayed.

The message from Betty Hardin did not make things any better. She would be arriving on the late-running stage and the Kid knew he could not hide his guilty secret from her. She would read his normally inscrutable face like a book and would demand to know all. The Kid did not know if he could face her, so he proposed to take the cowardly way out. No lady would enter a saloon when it was open for business so the Kid

would be safe here until Betty was asleep. That would
hold off the awful disclosure until the following morning, but he was not sure how Betty would take it even
then.

The batwing doors of the saloon opened and a man
entered. He stood just inside, allowing his eyes to
become used to the light, and studied the other patrons
of the bar. He was a stocky, handsome young man, his
face tanned, friendly and with a black moustache. His
expensive grey Stetson was shoved back to show his
crinkly, curly black hair. His clothes were range style,
expensive and pointed to a tophand. The gunbelt told
another story, it fitted well and hung just right. The
holster was cut to the shape of the gun, leaving the
triggerguard and most of the chamber exposed. It was
the holster of a fast gunhandler, leaving the ivory
handle, hammer and triggerguard of the Civilian Model
Peacemaker clear for easy gripping and lifting, and the
bottom was tied down. The average cowhand did not
wear such a holster, and rarely tied the tip down to hold
it against a fast draw. It was the holster of a real good
man and matched the one at Chris Madsen's side, or
Bent's or, to a lesser extent, the Ysabel Kid's.

The newcomer stood by the door, looking around
him. It was not the cold stare of a man hunting trouble,
but caution. His eyes took in the group at the bar, and a
warm, friendly smile came to his face as his eyes rested
on the Kid. Recognition was mutual.

"Yahoo!" the Kid whooped. "We done got our
baritone."

Chris Madsen's eyes were on the newcomer, the smile
still playing on his lips as the Kid advanced toward the
man with an outstretched hand. Madsen did not move
from the bar, but he stiffened slightly as he watched the
newcomer.

Letting out a wild cowhand yip, the new arrival
gripped the Kid's hand in a hearty shake. "Ain't see you
all in a coon's age, Lon," he whooped. "How you been

keeping? Where's Dusty and Mark?"

"Feel as fit as a flea," the Kid replied, flushing slightly as his conscience pricked him. "You couldn't have come at a better time, S—"

"You're surely right, boy," interrupted the other man, drowning the Kid's voice. "I called in for a game of poker. Yes, sir, as sure as my name's *Eph Tenor*, I feel lucky tonight."

"Sorry we can't oblige you none, S—, Eph," Bent replied, advancing. He'd caught the slight emphasis on the name and read it correctly. "We've just been fixing to raise us a quartet. You want in on it?"

"Why sure," agreed Eph, his tone showing that he was another devotee to the art of quartet harmony. "Who all's singing second tenor?"

There was a grin on Bent's face as he led the newcomer to the bar. "Allow you two never met afore," he said. "This here's Chris Madsen, Eph. Chris, get acquainted with Eph Tenor, from Texas."

Eph's grin never wavered as he held out his hand to the United States Marshal. Nor did Madsen's face lose the smile as he eyed the other man. "Pleased to meet you – Eph. You up this way on business?"

"Me?" grinned Eph. "Shucks no. Just came along to see if I could do a mite of hoss racing. I've got me a little mare out there that can run a quarter faster'n most hoss's can cover a hundred yards."

There was a pause, then Madsen chuckled. "Any particular town in mind?"

"Nope, just juning around, looking for some place that'll be worth it."

Bent snorted. Time was passing; his quartet was complete and he wanted to start. "Come on," he insisted. "Pour out a drink for Eph, then let's give her a whirl."

With the dust washed from Eph's throat, Bent got them ready to move off with the first song. He waved his hand to the Kid and suggested that he start with "Little Joe the Wrangler."

For an impromptu group the quartet got on well. There was not a sound through the room as the few customers and the girls from the dancehall listened. The four voices worked in well; Madsen's second tenor, Eph's baritone and Bent's bass giving able backing.

There was some applause from the listening crowd when the song came to an end, and Madsen took over with the sad ballad of "My Darling Clementine." Then Eph's baritone gave the lead in the lament of a dying cowhand.

The song was just at the crucial point when the doors of the bar opened and a party of weary, footsore men entered.

Eph's song died as Bent lunged forward from the bar toward the men at the door. He recognized the driver and guard of the late stagecoach. Recognized them, and knew they were in trouble, for he'd not heard the coach arrive.

"What's happened, Scotty?" he snapped.

"Been held up," replied the guard. "They took off with that young gal who was traveling with us."

The Ysabel Kid left the bar and crossed the room fast, his face no longer young and innocent looking. The guard gulped and took a pace aback. He was a brave man, good with his weapons and used to taking care of himself in times of trouble, but that black-dressed boy looked meaner and more dangerous than a cow moose defending her new-born calf. "What gal was that?" he growled.

"Miss Hardin," the driver replied for the guard. "Ole Devil Hardin's granddaughter. She – hell fire, Ole Devil's gal! There'll be hell on over this."

"Mister," growled the Kid, his voice sounding like a Comanche taking a lodge oath of vengeance. "That hell's going to break loose a damned sight sooner than you expect. What happened?"

The businessman pushed forward glaring wildly around the room. His eyes lit on Chris Madsen, but, despite his earlier remarks, he did not appear to recognize the United States marshal.

"It was the James gang!" the businessman yelled.

"The James gang?" Madsen remarked. He'd been eyeing Eph with some interest but turned and crossed the room, digging his badge from his pocket. "Are you sure of that?"

"The leader was a big man," put in the drummer eagerly, not wishing to be left out of the limelight. "Six-foot three or four at least, and mean looking—"

"Weren't they masked?" Madsen asked, then turned to Eph who was putting his hat on. "Don't go yet, Eph. We'll be doing some more singing when I've tended to this."

"Of course they was masked," replied the drummer heatedly. "You should have seen that Jesse James. Big! – He was at least six-foot four and his eyes were black. Coldest eyes I ever saw, they just seemed to go right through a man."

"You sure it was Jesse James?" Madsen went on, glancing back to Eph.

"One of them called him Jesse," the businessman answered, wanting to get the attention back to himself once more. "There were at least ten of them in the gang and the guard didn't dare do a thing against them."

Madsen looked up at the roof, as if searching for strength to carry on. The Ysabel Kid turned to the guard, about to ask how Betty Hardin was taken without a fight. Madsen could read the signs and wanted to keep things peaceable, so he looked at the passengers and said:

"You gents best go to the bar and get a drink, after all that danger you've been in."

"May I ask who you are?" inquired the businessman pompously.

"Madsen, U.S. Marshal."

"Then, sir, may I ask how a gang like the James brothers could be allowed to operate in Oklahoma

Territory, robbing and plundering. It's an outrage, sir; I was robbed of a considerable sum—"

"I'll see Marshal Thomas about it, sir," Madsen replied, hiding a grin. "He handles the James gang. You wouldn't want me to get into no jurisdictional trouble with him, would you?"

The businessman snorted, but turned and followed the other passengers to the bar. There, surrounded by an eager audience, he forgot his principles and stood with a glass of whisky in his hand, telling all and sundry about his narrow escape. There was a considerable difference in the descriptions the three men gave of the outlaws and none was accurate enough to help in the search.

"All right," growled the Kid. "Tell it!"

"Jesse James!" Madsen snorted. "Why does every witness in a holdup have to insist it was Jesse James?"

Eph wandered over looking interested. "You sure it couldn't have been old Dingus then?"

"I never forget the description of *any* wanted man, Eph," replied Madsen. "A big man, over six-foot, wide shouldered, with mean black eyes – pah! Jesse James's slim built, five-foot ten and his eyes are light blue. That description don't even tally with Cole Younger, or any of the James gang."

"Who were they, Scotty?" Bent asked the guard.

"Bunch of buttons, likely on their first chore, which is why I took no chances with them. I didn't like the look of that boy leading 'em. Seemed he might go hawg-wild and start shooting if there was trouble. That's why I didn't stack in when they were taking Miss Hardin with them. She warned me off: I was set to make a go, but she signaled me not to do it."

That figured to the Kid: Betty knew gunmen. She'd know that help was at Bent's Ford and would go along with the outlaws. The Kid suddenly felt better. If he'd stayed with his friends there would be no one here to go help Betty.

"If they lay a hand on that gal," he growled savagely, "I'll—"

"Ease down, Kid," Scotty answered, recognizing the young man now. "They won't harm her none. They're gentlemen owlhoots. Just out of a story book, robbing the rich to give to the poor. Why, they gave that there nester some money out of the take, 'cause he didn't have much. Didn't take me'n Wheeler's guns with 'em when we said we bought them. They won't hurt her none – unless they get scared."

Ysabel Kid led out his breath in a long gust. He thought of Betty Hardin as a well-loved sister and swore he'd not rest until she was free. If those owlhoots had harmed her in any way they'd learn how a quarter-Comanche boy acted when he got riled. He could rely on the guard's judgment of the men. They would treat Betty well enough as long as they weren't spooked and their pose as gentlemen outlaws wasn't shattered.

"Where'd it happen?" he asked.

"Five-mile out. Scattered our team and left us afoot. You can't find their line in the dark, Kid."

"Scotty's right, Lon," Madsen agreed. "How many were there in the gang, Scotty?"

"Five," answered the guard, grinning as he heard the whisky drummer telling a couple of enthralled girls and a young cowhand how he'd have stopped the holdup if there had not been eighteen men in the gang.

"Won't need a big posse then," remarked Madsen thoughtfully. "It'd be best if we didn't take too many men. If we come on that gang they might get scared."

"Wonder how they aim to send the ransom note," Scotty said as he turned to leave the saloon. "Might help you, if you lose their trail."

The doors closed behind the driver and guard as they headed for the Wells Fargo office to make their reports of the incident. Madsen stood for a moment, looking thoughtful. He could see there was no need to send telegraph messages; the fewer men hunting the gang the safer it would be for Betty Hardin.

"I'll take you along, Kid," he said; then, as if as an after-thought: "You'd best ride along, Eph."

Eph scratched his jaw. "Waal, happen it's all the same to you, and there ain't no great danger to Miss Hardin, I'd as soon be left out."

"Can't do it, Eph," replied Madsen gently. "All these gents here are hidebound for some place urgent and you allow to be just juning around. Legislation of the Oklahoma Territory says a duly appointed officer can deputize any man. It means a spell in pokey to refuse and you wouldn't want that to happen. We might have to wire your home town and let them know."

Eph's smile faded, his face tightened and his hand dropped to his belt, only inches from his gun butt. Chris Madsen's eyes never left the Texan's face, but his fingers spread slightly, hovering near the butt of his gun. Then slowly Eph relaxed, the grin came back and he was once more the happy-go-lucky cowhand who'd earlier sung in the quartet.

"Wouldn't want to put you to all that trouble, Chris," he drawled easily. "It might be inconvenient but I'll go along with you. Allus did say there was a nasty, mean streak in tenors though. The Kid's another one."

"Sure," replied Madsen, also relaxing. "I'll stable your hosses in the barn with mine tonight. Wouldn't want to wake up and find them gone, would we?"

With that, Madsen turned back to the bar. Eph met the Kid's sardonic gaze and grinned wryly. "I'll tell you, Lon, that's a tolerable smart lawman."

Bent relaxed; nothing could be done until morning so he could get on with some more singing. His quartet gathered at the bar, keeping clear of the holdup victims who were still telling of their experience.

"Know something, Chris?" said the Kid, as he leaned his elbow on the bar. "I feel sorry for that bunch."

The words carried to the other party and a girl asked

what the Kid meant. It was the businessman who replied. He'd taken a few whisky slugs and felt ready to head out and handle the gang without help. He focused his eyes on the Kid, no easy matter, for the Kid appeared to be spinning around with the rest of the room.

"What he means, my dear," he said wisely, "is that he's sorry for that poor young lady, helpless, defenseless, in the hands of those bloodthirsty desperadoes."

"I tell you, boys," drawled the Kid to the other members of the quartet, "he don't know lil ole Betty Hardin. Let's give Barbara Allen a whirl, shall we?"

The following morning at the first light of dawn, the Ysabel Kid was out saddling his big white stallion. He slid the Winchester rifle into the saddleboot and checked that a full box of Winchester .44 rimfire bullets, his powder flask, bullet bag and percussion caps were in his saddlepouch. He was leaving his bedroll with Bent to lighten the load on his horse. Near at hand Chris Madsen and Eph Tenor were also preparing for the ride and Bent stood by with packages of food.

"Dusty and Mark might be along today," the Kid said as he swung astride the white horse. "Tell them what's happened and to wait here until they hear from me."

The three men rode off along the stage trail while Bent watched them. He felt sorry for the holdup gang, matched against the combined talents of the three men.

The stage coach was where it was left the previous day, for the Wells Fargo men wanted to let the posse search the ground before bringing in a new team and messing the sign up. Chris Madsen halted his horse and nodded to the Kid, who swung down from his saddle and went forward, his eyes on the ground. Madsen could read sign well, but he knew that the Kid could make him look a learner in the art.

The Kid examined the ground with great care; Betty

Hardin's life and safety depended on his skill. There was much he could read from the dust at the edge of the trail and the grass crushed down by feet; there little that he missed. He could guess how tall each member of the gang was and even recognized boot prints.

"One thing's for sure," he said, mounting the horse with a quick, Indian-like bound. "They aren't experts, that's for sure. And they haven't done much of this work, or if they have, it hasn't paid them."

"How'd you know, Kid?" Eph asked.

"Easy, their boots are run over at the heels, one pair looks like it's damned near worn clean through. They'd have bought new boots had they been in the money. Hosses aren't much either, sore-footed bunch from the looks of their sign. We can run them down if we catch up on them."

" 'Cepting they've got Miss Hardin, so we can't," reminded Eph. "Looks like they've left some clear sign for you."

"That's what worries me," replied the Kid. "They're playing at being real smart owlhoots. They'll have some game worked out for throwing us off their tracks."

The sign was plain enough to allow them to make fair time following it. The Kid rode at the head of the party, Eph following and Madsen bringing up the rear. They did not speak as they rode but all were alert. The way of working was standard. The man following the sign would give it his full attention while the other two kept a careful lookout for possible ambush. There was not much danger of ambush as yet, but none of the three believed in taking foolish risks. The gang they were after would be well ahead, but there were other outlaws around who might take an aggressive attitude to the posse.

For once in his life the Ysabel Kid was anxious and worried. Although Betty Hardin was a cool, capable young lady, she was outnumbered by the gang. She'd have sense enough to go along without causing any trouble, knowing that help was coming.

The Kid brought his horse to a halt as they approached the rocky land. His eyes took in the crushed grass: the party had stopped here and got down from their horses. He looked around, then stiffened as a small black object lying on the ground caught his eyes.

"Tracks go off that ways, Kid," Eph remarked.

"Why sure," agreed the Kid. "There ain't but one of 'em being rid, rest are led. Look how close they're together. Men wouldn't ride all bunched up like that. 'Sides, there ain't but the five hosses going off."

"Rest took to the rocks then, Kid," Madsen said. "Make it harder for us. How do you call it, stick after the five or try and trail the gang over the rocks?"

"Stick after the gang. They'll have to leave this rock some place. The one with the spare hosses'll make good time across the range, then scatter them. We'd wind up following one lone man, which is harder than trailing a bunch."

"Which way'd they go over the rock then?" asked Eph, looking down at the hard ground and seeing nothing to help him.

"Their spare hosses would have to be left in that outcrop there," Madsen guessed. "We could try and pick up their line over the way, Lon."

"Why sure," agreed the Kid, walking forward. He bent and picked up the glove Betty had dropped, a grin flickering across his face.

At the outcrop the Kid went over the ground again, learning all he could, but it was not much. He estimated how long the horses were left, which was easy enough from the droppings left behind. Then he started following the trail over ground which gave little sign, even of six horses. It was a slow business but the Kid was painstaking.

"Hell, this'll spoil things for us, Lon," Madsen growled, as they came in sight of the rocky-bottomed, fast-running stream.

They halted on the banks and looked at the stream. The trail ended at the edge of the water, without any hint as to whether the riders crossed straight over, went up or downstream.

The Kid sat his horse, listening to the sound of the stream running over the rocky bed. His attention was on the sound as he heard Madsen speaking.

"Up or down, do you reckon, Eph?"

"I wouldn't know. Never had a chance to be at this end of a – mean I never rode in a posse afore."

"I'd near on bct upstream," the Kid said finally.

"Any reason for it?" enquired Madsen.

"Listen," replied the Kid. "There's some real fast water, likely a waterfall, near to hand. They went downstream and they'd have to come out again before it'd be worth it."

The other two listened, faintly catching the noise of rushing, falling water above the sound of the stream before them. Both felt admiration at the way the Kid heard, recognized, and saw the importance of the sound.

"Would you reckon they'd know about it?" asked Madsen.

"Likely. They know this country. They planned this whole thing out in advance, even to losing us here on the stream. They'd get here just afore dark, way I see it. Wouldn't take no chances of breaking a hoss's leg in the dusk."

With that the Kid rode into the water, heading upstream; the others followed him. It was easy to follow the bed of the stream, and they splashed on until they came to some branches partially hanging over the water. The Kid saw the second glove and showed it to the other two, then slipped it with its mate in his pocket. Then he looked at the tip of a branch and leaned forward to scrape the horse hairs from it. Ignoring the other two he carefully separated the different-colored hairs, peering at them as they lay in his palm.

"Make it a bay, couple or so roans, a black and a couple of duns," he said, passing the hairs back to Madsen, who confirmed the colors. "Be a mite of help, happen we catch up."

Eph was watching everything with undisguised interest. "You mean you can tell all this, just by reading sign and finding hoss hair?"

"Why sure," Madsen replied. "Except there aren't another ten men in the West who can read sign like the Kid. I reckon to be fair, so's Billy and Heck, but we're yearly beef compared with the Kid."

The horses started forward once more, the Kid watching the banks of the stream. He was trying to work out how long the gang had stayed in the water. They would come ashore before it was dark which would bring them out somewhere along the stretch they were now following.

A flutter of white caught the Kid's eyes. At the same moment the Kid saw marks on the bank where the horses had left and he turned the head of his white toward it. Swinging down from the saddle he picked up the handkerchief and slid it into his bulging pocket. He glanced at the sun; it was now long past noon.

"Let's take a bit of Bent's chow,' he suggested. "Let the hosses blow."

So they halted on the banks of the stream, loosening the saddle girths and allowing the horses to drink, then browse on the stunted vegetation at the side of the stream. The men ate their meal in silence, then sat smoking for a time, allowing the horses to rest. At last Madsen came to his feet, stubbed out his cigarette and went to his horse.

The tracking was resumed; slowly they worked over the ground in the direction taken by the gang. Then they reached easy ground and the speed of their trailing picked up. For all that, the sun was down when they brought their horses to a halt on a stage trail.

"This's a hell of a note," Madsen grunted. "There's

a small town down that way, they'd likely go the other direction.''

The Kid did not agree. ''They've been swinging the other way all the time and their line was headed up-trail when they came off.''

''If they kept to this trail they'd have to pass through the town ahead,'' objected Madsen. ''They wouldn't want to risk it, not having Miss Hardin along.''

''It'd be getting on two, three o'clock at least when they come through. Sure wouldn't meet many folks at that time,'' answered the Kid. ''They'd chance it and we'd have to be real lucky to find their line again if they stick to the trail for any distance.''

Madsen nodded. There was something in what the Kid said. He turned his horse and headed toward the small town. The other two followed him now. He was the U.S. marshal and in command of the posse, it was his place to lead them. In the town he could ask around and find out if anyone had heard riders passing through in the night. He had the authority to ask and would get the answers.

They rode into the main street. It was empty and deserted, for most of the citizens were at dinner, in their homes after closing their business or finishing work. The saloon's windows were lit but only three horses stood hip-shot at the hitching rail.

Madsen was looking for some sign of the marshal's office but saw none as they rode along the street. He gave the three horses a casual glance and would have ridden on but the Kid caught his arm.

''We made us a hit,'' the Kid said and his voice showed more excitement than was usual. ''Bay and roan hoss . . .''

''There's a hell of a lot of both in the Indian Nations,'' Madsen replied.

''Sure, but that bay's favoring his off-hind a mite, like one we've been on the trail of all day.''

Madsen looked down at the bay, noting the way it

was keeping weight off its right hind leg. It could be a coincidence but they'd little to go on. He swung his horse to the hitching rail and dismounted, tossed the reins over the rail, then ducked around his horse to look the bay over. Behind him the Kid and Eph were also dismounting. The Kid went around his white horse and was about to join Madsen when he stopped, looking at the saddle on the washy sorrel.

"I'll take money these are what we're after," he remarked casually. "Take me for a ten spot, Chris?"

"I'll take you," Madsen replied, grinning. He could not lose on the bet. If the Kid was wrong the ten-dollar bet would be his, if the Kid was right they'd got part of the gang and that was worth the ten spot.

Without another word the Kid went to the sorrel, reaching up behind the cantle. Then extended a hand to Madsen, holding a woman's overnight bag in it. Madsen looked at the two sets of silver initials on the bag; BH and OD, the O touching the straight side of the D.

"You saw it," he growled.

"And you didn't," replied the unsympathetic Kid, holding out his other hand.

"I'll pay you when we get through."

"Oh no," drawled the Kid. "My pappy allus used to tell me, 'Trust in the Lord, but make other folks pay their gambling debts right off.'"

Madsen grinned, handing over two five-dollar pieces which the Kid slid away. Then they both went to the window. There was not much to see: a few men sitting at tables and three youngsters wearing cowhand clothes, lounging at the bar. They were a poorly dressed trio, but even as the posse watched, one of them pulled a ten-dollar bill from a roll and paid for a round of drinks.

"They're our boys," Eph said eagerly. "Cowhands as poor looking as them shouldn't have all that money."

"Let's make some talk," Madsen replied.

The three youngsters at the bar, and the rest of the

customers studied the new arrivals with interest, for their town saw few strangers. The three youngsters at the bar started drunkenly, their eyes focusing on the marshal's badge Madsen wore pinned to his calfskin vest. The whisky died in them, leaving only a cold, scared feeling in their stomachs. It was plain they were guilty men.

Chris Madsen was a trained law officer. He knew the rules for approaching a suspect and watched the three young men all the time. They might not be the men he was looking for, but they were scared at the sight of his badge and a scared man was every bit as dangerous as a hardened killer. So they gave all their attention to the youngsters at the bar. Not one of them noticed a whiskered, hard-faced man who sat with his back to the wall, near the door. He gave Chris Madsen a hard look and dropped his hand out of sight behind the table, glanced at the door and gently eased his chair back, preparing to come to his feet.

Madsen halted in front of the three youngsters, his hand hanging by the butt of his gun ready to draw. He sensed that the Ysabel Kid was just as ready at his left side and wondered what Eph was doing at his right.

"You boys done much riding?" he asked.

"Who wants to know?" Ben asked, the whisky making him tough.

"Chris Madsen, U.S. Marshal," Madsen introduced himself.

Eph was not paying much attention to the three youngsters, knowing Madsen and the Kid could handle them. He glanced in the bar mirror and saw the bearded man coming from the chair, his gun lining on the marshal's back. Eph's left hand shot out, thrusting Madsen violently to one side and sending him staggering behind the Kid. The bearded man's shot crashed out, the bullet making a hole in the bar between Sam and Jube. Eph turned, his right hand lashing down as he moved, the Ivory-handled Colt swinging up ready. When he was fully around, his left hand fanned the hammer. The three shots came so fast they sounded as one continuous roll, the bearded man took the lead. He spun around, crashed into the wall and slid down, his gun falling from his hand as he went.

The Ysabel Kid never accounted himself fast with a gun, for it took him all of a second to draw and shoot his old Dragoon. A fast man could halve that time and kill at the end. He caught a glimpse of what was happening, saw the three young men starting to move toward their guns. His palm twisted outward, caught the worn walnut grips of his old gun and lifted the Dragoon from leather. His thumb cocked the hammer and he threw down on the three youngsters long before they moved. He picked Ben out as the most dangerous and the yawning muzzle of the old cap and ball .44 lined on his stomach.

"Freeze fast and solid!" growled the Kid.

Madsen landed on his hands and knees; he rolled over, gun coming out to line first at Eph, then on the three young men at the bar. The trio of outlaws were standing as if frozen, for Eph turned to line his Colt on them and augment the Kid.

Slowly Madsen came to his feet, he'd seen the crumpled body of the bearded man and knew what must have happened. "Thanks, Sam," he said to Eph. "Lordy, a man who's worn a law badge for all the years I have, falling for a trick like that."

"He warn't with us, Marshal!" Jube yelped nervously. "Honest to Henry, we never saw him afore."

"Pull their teeth, Lon," Madsen replied. He could tell the young outlaw was speaking the truth. The man was not one of them and they'd no part in the attempt on his life. "Where were you bunch yesterday?"

"Why you accusing us honest folks for, Marshal?" demanded Ben, trying to hold his voice tough and hard, though he had no gun now.

"Figger you might know something about the stage

that was held up yesterday," replied Madsen, watching the townspeople through the bar mirror, then glancing at the bartender as he came into view after diving for safety when the shooting commenced.

"We warn't nowheres near Bent's Ford yesterday," Ben answered, then stopped and his face lost its color.

"How'd you know the coach was held up near Bent's then?" snapped Madsen. "I'm taking you in for it."

The batwing doors were tossed open and a fat man stepped in, a ten-gauge shotgun in his hands. He was a jovial, leisurely looking individual wearing old cavalry trousers and a collarless shirt. Holding the batwing doors open he let the light shine on the bearded man, then stepped in through the door. The shotgun was held with careless competence, like he knew well enough how to handle it.

"Who'd have done this?" he asked in a lazy drawl.

"One of my posse," Madsen replied. "Man was all set to gun me from behind. I'm Madsen, U.S. Marshal."

"Name's Jeffers, Constable and Marshal of Trimble," introduced the fat man coming forward. "Would you know this gent, Marshal?"

Madsen crossed and looked down. He bent over and made a closer examination, then straightened and nodded. "I know him. It's Dutch Charlie. Used to run with the Doolin gang until Bill kicked him out. Took him a lodge oath to get Billy Tilghman Heck and me." He looked across the room toward his posse men. "I'm obliged, S . . . Eph. I'm not sorry to see the end of him."

"Wondered some about him," the constable of the town said thoughtfully. "He come in quiet enough, troubled nobody. Would have spotted him if it wasn't for the whiskers. What's wrong with the other three?"

"Do you know them?"

"Seen them and two more hanging around here.

Thought they worked for one of the cattle outfits. Never had much money . . .''

"They got plenty tonight, Slim,'' called the bartender. "All of 'em bought drinks and changed a ten spot each. Peeled it right off a roll.''

Madsen nodded. The young fools could not resist flashing their money, never realizing they were giving themselves away by doing it. He explained what the three were suspected of but the constable was unable to help in any way.

"Where'd you get the money?'' Madsen asked, returning to the bar.

"Picking blueberries,'' Ben sneered.

The Kid moved forward, his face hard and savage. "Face the bar!'' he ordered.

There was something in the Kid's face which made Ben obey. It sank through the whisky fog which whirled in his head that here was a man who aimed to be obeyed. It was all very well to fool around and give lip to a lawman who was bound by certain rules as to how he treated his prisoners. This black-dressed Texan was no lawman; he was not the sort to care for rules either and would be quite willing to use his old Dragoon Colt or his bowie knife to enforce his orders. With this in mind Ben turned and faced the bar.

The Kid went forward, caught Ben's leg and lifted it to look at the sole of his boot, then raised the other leg. Letting go of Ben, the Kid went along the bar and looked at the other two pairs of boots. The heels of each pair were badly run over and he recognized them from the marks he'd seen during his trailing. But they were not what he was looking for. The pair of boots which were almost worn through had not shown to his inspection.

"Where's your pards?'' the Kid asked.

"We don't know what you're talking about,'' Ben answered; then he remembered something he'd heard said by a man arrested by a marshal. "I want to see a lawyer before I say another word!"

"Where do you hold prisoners, Constable?" Madsen asked.

"Don't often have none. When I do they go in the cellar under my house. We're a poor town and don't run to a jail. If I get a prisoner anytime I send word to the County Seat and they come over to collect him."

The Kid was looking thoughtful. "Know, Chris," he drawled, "we don't have a hell of a lot we can hold this bunch with." He winked at Eph who was watching him with some interest. "Nope, we couldn't hold them on much at all. Tell you, turn 'em loose one at a time. Me 'n' Eph here'll just take this one out and see him on his way."

Before Chris Madsen could say a word, the Kid and Eph took hold of Ben's arm and hustled him out into the night. Sim and Jube watched their friend go, then exchanged scared looks. They did not know what to make of this treatment and wished they'd Joe or Jesse with them.

Suddenly, from outside there sounded a most hideous scream; the scream of a man in mortal pain, then it died off to a gurgling moan and ended. Madsen and the constable stared at the door and two young outlaws lost all their color. The citizens in the saloon came to their feet. Every eye was on the door and Madsen forgot his prisoners as he stepped forward to investigate.

The batwing doors opened to admit the Ysabel Kid. His bowie knife was in his grip, he wiped the blade on his trouser leg and grinned at the startled faces.

"What the hell happened, Kid?" Madsen asked, voice hoarse and worried. "What was that scream?"

"He got stubborn, wouldn't be sociable and talk," replied the Kid with a blood-chilling chuckle. "Turn the next one loose. Best make it the chubby one, I don't want to spoil my knife's edge by hitting bone. Not when there's another one who'll need her, happen chubby don't tell us where the other two and Betty are."

Chris Madsen did not know what to do or say. He knew the Ysabel Kid's reputation very well and knew a little about the man called Eph Tenor. It was quite possible, if all the stories were true, that he'd used that bowie knife on the young outlaw. Madsen gulped and saw the town's constable looking pale around the gills. That scream was enough to make any man look and act that way.

Jube opened his mouth and let out a yell of pure terror as the Kid advanced across the floor toward him. "Don't let him get me," he howled. "Keep him off. We done that stage job but we never hurt nobody. We didn't harm the gal, she's out at our hideout."

"Where'd that be?" asked the Kid, casually flipping the razor-edged bowie knife from hand to hand.

"An old farm couple of miles north of here. It was empty when we got there and we moved in."

"That'd be the old Miller place," the constable put in. "They pulled out for the East and left most of their gear at the farm."

Madsen knew the youngster was not lying: he was too scared. The marshal was pleased to get the information, but worried as to the means by which it was obtained. He licked his lips worriedly and looked at the Kid but could read nothing in that innocent, inscrutable face. He wondered how he would explain away a prisoner, unarmed, yet killed with the knife of one of the posse.

In every community there were a section of people who boasted they were for the rights of the working man and set out to prove it by looking for anything detrimental or damaging to the reputation of the Army, Navy or law enforcement officers of the land. There was such a body in Oklahoma, a thorn in the flesh of the governor and every lawman in the territory. The killing of an unarmed prisoner would really give this body a thing to get their teeth and claws in. Chris Madsen would be lucky if he was only thrown out of office.

"What the hell happened out there, Kid?" he finally managed to growl.

"Out where?" countered the Kid, mildly innocent.

"What was that yell?" Madsen's voice rose a shade.

"Was there a yell?" asked the Kid.

"You know there was!" Madsen yelled.

"You mean a yell like this?" replied the Kid. He opened his mouth; from it came the same hideous scream of pain, then a gurgle as if the throat was filling with blood.

For a long moment Madsen did not reply. He, and every other man in the room, stood staring at the Ysabel Kid, hardly believing that a living man could make such a sound.

At last Madsen found his voice. "Then it was you and not—!"

There was sardonic amusement in the Kid's voice as he replied, "Why sure. What else did you reckon it might have been? You didn't allow I'd struck ole Annie Breen here," he gestured with the bowie knife, "into that young feller we took outside, did you?"

"Dealing with a damned crazy Comanche like you a man doesn't know what the hell to think," Madsen snorted. "Where the hell is he?"

"S . . . Eph's got him out there. Keeping him quiet."

There came a scuffling and a thud from outside the saloon. The batwing doors burst open and Ben came in backward, crashing to the floor with his legs waving feebly. Eph stepped in, rubbing his knuckles, and grinning at the young outlaw. Outside Ben had suddenly been overcome with a desire to depart for new pastures and had attempted to bring this about by knocking Eph down. It was not a success for Eph's left hand parried the wild swing Ben launched, shoving it harmlessly away from him. Then his entirely unwild right fist shot out and knocked Ben through the door, for he was no mean hand at knocking down.

"Reckon we'd best take these three to your cellar and get Dutch Charlie hauled to your undertaker's shop," Madsen said to the constable. "I'd best get the three boys under lock and key before anything else happens. I'm holding them for stage robbery – kidnapping as well – they took a young woman off the stage."

"And I surely wish we hadn't," Sam wailed. "That gal's enough to turn a man offen women for ever. She had us sweeping and cleaning everything up. Made us wash and shave afore she'd let us eat at the table and bawled me out for eating beans offen a knife. We had her another week and we'd have been paying Ole Devil Hardin to take her back again."

The Kid grinned. It seemed Betty was all right. She affected the hands at the OD Connected the same way when she was in one of her moods. The thing now was to rescue Betty before the other two outlaws started worrying about their friends.

"Ain't much room for three prisoners in the cellar," remarked the constable. "But I don't reckon they'll want to walk about much."

"Where's this farm, friend?" asked the Kid of the bartender, watching Madsen and the constable escorting the three young outlaws out of the saloon.

"Just following the trail north a piece, and you'll come to a path leading off to the left. The farm's about a mile along it."

"How'd you reckon to get up to it, Kid?" Eph asked. "Move in on foot?"

"I daren't chance it. Nope, I've got me an idea that might work out. Happen Chris'll agree and our friend behind the bar can get us a hat and a pile of blankets. Hope Chris ain't took their hosses with him. Take a look, Sam; if he has, get them back."

"Want any of us along?" asked the bartender eagerly.

"Admire to have you, friend," replied the Kid. "But

they're holding a gal prisoner and they'd likely hurt her if they heard a crowd coming. The leader of the gang's still out there and he's a boy who'll spook if things go wrong.''

"See what you mean. We'll stand out and leave it to you. I hope you can get the gal out without her being hurt.''

"Mister," said the Kid grimly and sincerely. "So do I.''

"I shaw a big-pig Yankee marshal comin' down the shtreet.
Got two Dragoon guns in hish belt, looks fiersh enough to eat.
Now big-pig Yankee stay away. Stay right, clear of me.
I'm a lil boy from Texshus and scared ash I can be – hic!

Joe listened to the drunken voice and pulled aside the curtains to peer out into the night. He could see a rider approaching leading three horses, the three horses his friends rode to town. Across each saddle was a shape that looked like a body. He felt scared until he saw the rider swing down from his big black horse, stagger and almost fall, and clinging to the saddle for support.

"Hello the housh!!" the man yelled, staggering toward the porch and swinging up on to it with a whisky-soddened abandon. "Anybody home?"

"Who is it?" Joe asked, glancing at Jesse who was still holding Betty.

"Me!" replied the voice with drunken logic, then a puzzled note took its place, "Leasht I think it's me. Hey, you three, is this one of you up here, and me down there on the hoss?" There was a pause. "Naw, it can't be. Come on, open up. Your pardsh allowed there'd be something to drink here.''

Joe grinned and reached for the door handle. It was

just like Ben and the other two to get drunk and make friends with a stranger, then have to be brought home across their saddles. They must have told the stranger where to come before they'd collapsed under the load of coffin-varnish. It would be safe to open the door, for the man who'd brought Ben and the others back did not sound or look in much better condition than they were.

Holstering his gun Joe opened the door. Instantly a hand shot out, gripping his throat; something hard, cold and round was thrust savagely under his chin and he was forced backward into the room. The most savage face he'd ever seen loomed before his startled eyes and he croaked a scared yell.

The Ysabel Kid forced Joe backward into the room, holding his throat with the left hand while the right forced the muzzle of the Dragoon Colt under Joe's chin. The Kid's thumb held the hammer back and the trigger was depressed ready to fire. Then he saw Jesse and Betty. He saw the way the young outlaw held Betty, saw the knife so near her face and the fear in the man's eyes.

"Hold it!" Jesse yelled and there was near panic in his voice. "I'll kill the girl if you don't let go of Joey."

The Kid made no move to release Joe. His eyes went first to Jesse, then to the girl. Betty was cool enough, standing without moving and making no attempt to struggle against Jesse's grip. She met the Kid's gaze and almost imperceptibly she nodded her head. But the Kid was annoyed. He'd made a fool mistake. A bunch like this would go in for dramatic things like signal whistles when approaching the hideout. He should have thought of it earlier and got the signal from one of the prisoners. They'd have told him, for, according to Chris Madsen, they were talking plenty, confessing their few crimes since becoming a band of outlaws.

"Give it up," drawled the Kid evenly. "We've got the place surrounded and you can't get out."

"I've got the gal!" Jesse answered, his voice pitched high and the knife hand moving spasmodically.

"And I've got your boy," warned the Kid. "Put the knife down."

"No!" Jesse yelled back. "I've got the gal. I'm going out of here an you ain't stopping me. Turn Joey loose."

It was a stand-off, although Jesse held slightly the stronger hand. The Kid could not shoot Joe, even though he was quite willing to do so. There was no moral scruple involved. If Betty had been in no danger he would not have hesitated, the gun would have rocked, throwing its round lead ball through Joe's head. That could not happen, not while the knife was so near to Betty's face.

"All right," he said, watching Betty's head bob in another quick nod. "You win, *hombre*."

The Kid shoved Joe to one side but did not holster his gun. Jesse saw his brother released and relaxed his hold, the knife moved away from Betty's neck. It was what she'd been waiting for. Back lashed her right foot, the Kelly spur driving into Jesse's shin and bringing a wild yell of pain from him. His grip relaxed and Betty's hands shot up to catch the arm which was round her shoulder. She gripped it and heaved; Jesse felt his feet leave the floor, the room whirled around and he landed with a crash on the hard boards. His Colt had fallen from his holster and he grabbed for it. Something cold touched his cheek; he turned his head into the muzzle of a short-barreled Merwin & Hulbert revolver in Betty's right hand.

"I've had it all the time, Jesse," she said. "You've heard tell of a shoulder clip, I reckon. You would have if you'd tried to touch me."

Joe clawed at his gun, then froze as he saw the Kid's Dragoon lined on him. Feet thudded on the porch and two men came in. Joe's grin died as he saw the men were strangers. He looked at the marshal's badge on Chris Madsen's vest, and the gun in Eph's hand. They'd been two of the "drunks" lying over Ben, Sam and Jube's saddles; the third "man" was on the rear horse, a roll of blankets with a hat fastened to it.

The Kid grinned at Betty. She'd sand to burn, that girl. Old Tommy Okasi's wrestling throws served Betty as well as they did Dusty Fog, when needed. The Kid stepped forward to kick Jesse's gun into the corner and saw Betty staring at Eph.

"Heavens to Betsy!" gasped Betty, recognition showing on her face. "It's Sa—"

Quickly the Kid gave Betty an ungentlemanly nudge in the ribs which ended her words. "This here's Eph Tenor, Betty gal," he said pointedly, then lowered his voice. "I know him, you know him, and Chris knows him. But Chris don't want it known he's been riding with Sam Bass for a day and never arrested him."

Betty smiled, the sort of smile which would have melted a miser's heart but did not fool the Ysabel Kid. Betty Hardin was getting set to charm her way. She felt sorry for the five young outlaws and knew that Chris Madsen took his prisoners for trial to Fort Smith, where the notorious Judge Parker, the Hanging Judge, presided. If Jesse and his gang came for trial before Parker, they would be lucky to get away with their lives and they did not deserve death or a brutal sentence of imprisonment.

"I suppose you'll be taking them to Fort Smith, Marshal," Betty said and the Kid watched her, a grin coming to his face.

"Sure, Miss Hardin," agreed Madsen. "I doubt if they'll bother you again."

"Couldn't they be tried in the county where they did the holdup?" she asked.

"Could be. I suppose they could be put for trial locally but I'm supposed to take them to the Fort."

Now Jesse was looking scared, realizing for the first time the consequences of being an outlaw. He and Joe looked so pathetic that Betty knew she must save them from Judge Parker.

Putting on a manner which would charm a bird out of

a tree, Betty smiled at Madsen. "You couldn't do me a small favor?"

"I don't know as I could, ma'am. They need teaching a lesson and . . ."

The Ysabel Kid's grin expanded. He knew how Betty Hardin operated, the trap was going to spring closed on Madsen.

"I was just thinking," said Betty innocently, "how folks would laugh if they heard the United States marshal, Chris Madsen, was riding for a full day with Sa—, Eph Tenor, and didn't recognize him. Of course none of us would want it to get out, but I declare that at times I just talk and talk."

"All right," Madsen answered, giving up, as so many other men did when opposing Betty Hardin's will. "I'll hand them over to the local law and let them do the trying. Did they treat you all right?"

"Like perfect gentlemen," replied Betty and Jesse looked relieved. The girl turned to the Ysabel Kid and went on, "Where's Cousin Dusty and Mark?"

"They stopped on in Mulrooney," said the Kid, trying to hold his face immobile but knowing she could read his thoughts.

"Did they?" asked Betty thoughtfully. "Come on, Loncey Dalton Ysabel, tell me all about it!"

The Kid tried to avoid telling Betty his guilty secret but halfway back to the town, riding well behind the others so only Betty could hear, the story came out.

Up in Mulrooney a good friend's wife produced her first son and Dusty Fog, Mark Counter and the Ysabel Kid found themselves roped in for the christening. Then came the trouble. The friend's wife came from one of the more sober families of the town and cowhand clothes would definitely not be worn for such an important occasion. Dusty and Mark were used to wearing suits, town clothes, buttoned collars and ties. Mark, the Kid suspected, even liked wearing such clothes at times and Dusty accepted them. The breaking point came when the Kid found he was also expected to wear the rig. He spent a sleepless night trying to think of a way to avoid the indignity and decided on flight.

"Anyways," he finished defiantly, "happen I hadn't done it there wouldn't have been any of us at Bent's Ford to come help you."

It was the following morning. Outside the small town's saloon Chris Madsen and the constable were preparing to escort the outlaws to the county seat for trial. Madsen turned to Betty Hardin, the Ysabel Kid and Eph Tenor standing on the porch, their horses ready to take them to Bent's Ford.

"Was I you, Eph," Madsen said, holding his hand out toward the Texan, "I'd forget about . . . horse-racing . . . in the Nations. It wouldn't be safe at all. It's not the hoss race season and we wouldn't want to take folks away from their daily labors to start racing with you."

"You could be right at that," grinned Eph in reply. "I'll maybe see you again some time, Chris."

"I hope not," replied Madsen, smiling back. "Not professionally, anyways."

Betty watched the marshal's party riding out of the town; then she turned to the man they'd been calling Eph Tenor.

"Sam Bass," she said, "if you're not the living end. Riding with a United States marshal and acting all friendly like. Wasn't he fixing to arrest you?"

"Why sure," agreed the Texas outlaw, grinning broader than ever. "I tell you, Miss Hardin, it's fit to turn a Texas boy honest the way that man never forgets a face or a description. Sure, I allow he'd have arrested me, or tried."

"And you still stopped that *hombre* back-shooting Chris?" remarked the Kid.

"Surely so, Lon," replied Sam Bass. "You never know when we might want another tenor for a quartet."

PART III

Some Knowledge of the Knife

THE BUZZARDS CIRCLED on wide-spread wings, swooping and whirling high in the sky. Twice they began a descent, only to rise again unable to take the chance of landing by the still form which lay on the sand in the center of the dried up stream.

Finally the black birds took the chance and started a circular glide toward the earth, then with frantically beating wings fought back into the air. They went higher and higher, their powerful vision seeing the man who came riding along a trail through the woods, headed for the streambed.

The Ysabel Kid rode easily in the double-girthed saddle of his huge white stallion. He looked relaxed but was alert and watchful. It was a normal condition with the Kid, for he'd learned early a man must keep alert if he wanted to stay alive. His eyes picked up the circling buzzards but he thought little of the whirling birds. They were not unusual; the buzzard was part of the range country scavenger corps, picking the flesh from the bones of dead animals.

Only this time it was not an animal which lay dead.

The Kid brought his horse to a halt as he left the trees and saw the body lying on the sand. He reached down and drew the Winchester rifle from his saddleboot before he dismounted. The man was dead but there was need for caution. The death was neither natural, nor suicide, as the knife hilt sticking from the center of the black broadcloth coat showed. It was murder and the murderer might still be lurking around, ready to take exception to anyone showing an interest in the body.

The woods around the Kid were still and only the faint noises of birds or small creatures came to his keen ears. He motioned to the big horse to stay where it was and advanced cautiously toward the body.

The woods widened out here to what must have been a river but was now dry, a gash of yellow sand running through the green of the wooded country. Here might once have been a ford almost a hundred yards across. The body lay halfway out, face down, stiff and still.

Just as he was about to step on the sand the Kid halted. His eyes went to the sign on the ground. The place was a regular crossing and well marked with a variety of tracks but the Kid saw immediately that there was only one recent set; they were old and blurred, except the prints of a big, well-made horse. That was the horse the dead man must have rode. The Kid kept well clear of the sign, a purely natural instinct to avoid spoiling it.

When he reached the body, the Kid was pleased he'd kept clear. He stopped and looked around him, trying to make out what had happened. By the side of the body were marks where the big horse had suddenly reared, the dead man falling from the saddle and rolling to lay as he now did. There were tracks where the horse had run on again, but nothing more. There was neither hoof nor foot prints to show how the knife came to be there. Just the bare sand, the one set of tracks and the old marks, nothing more.

The Ysabel Kid could read sign and there were few with his skill. This sign was all wrong; that the Kid knew. He looked down at the body. In life he'd been a big, well-dressed, white-haired man, a man the Kid could remember. He did not need to turn the body over to know that here lay the person Ole Devil Hardin had sent him to help. It looked like the help was a mite late in coming.

"Sorry, Judge," he said gently. "I come as soon as we got word."

Bending down, the Kid examined the tracks of the dead man's horse, paying careful attention to their depth. What he found out made him even more puzzled and he straightened up to look back toward his horse. It was all of fifty yards away. The Kid shook his head and turned to bend over the body, his eyes on the hilt of the knife. It was a style he'd never seen before and he knew quite a bit about knives and knife-fighters. The hilt was round, smooth and without any guard. What the blade was like the Kid could not tell for it was buried out of sight in the back of the coat.

The big white horse snorted, throwing back its head and moving restlessly. The Kid looked up, lifting his rifle slightly, ready to throw it to his shoulder as he saw three riders approaching from the open land on the other side of the sand. The Kid stood tense and watchful, looking more Indian than white as he prepared to hunt cover and fight for his life. Then he relaxed and rested the rifle barrel on his shoulder. He removed his low-crowned, wide-brimmed black Stetson and waved it to attract the attention of the men, then walked to the edge of the sand to meet them.

They were three Texas cowhands, two tall, one shorter. Tanned, efficient-looking men whose range clothes showed they were competent workers. They each wore a gunbelt, but none showed them as being real fast hands. The Kid knew their type. Loyal, hard-working, hard-playing men. Right now there was no levity in their expressions, only cold suspicion for they recognized their boss. The smaller man was looking hard at the Kid, his hand hanging by his side; the other two riders dropped their palms to the grips of their Colts.

"You'd best hold the hosses here, gents," said the Kid, not moving his rifle from his shoulder. "No sense in spoiling the sign for when the sheriff comes."

The three men looked down at the Indian-dark young

man and read the signs as well as the Kid. Here was a man, hard and tough, despite his innocent-looking young face. That rifle was pointed harmlessly to the sky, but it could be brought into action easily enough, as could the old Dragoon Colt which was butt forward at his right side.

"That's Judge Hurley there," one of the taller men growled.

"Sure," agreed the Kid.

"He dead, Kid?" grunted the small man.

The Ysabel Kid felt relieved that Carney Lee recognized him. The small man was the Judge's foreman, had been even in the days when the Kid's father, Sam Ysabel, ran contraband on the Rio Grande and found the Judge a very good customer. That was several years back and the Kid wondered if he'd changed much. Lee could have replied to that question.

"He's dead," agreed the Kid. "Light down and take a look."

The two cowhands glanced at their foreman. He knew this dangerous-looking young Texan but they were not entirely satisfied. Carney Lee swung from his horse and, as the other two dismounted, introduced them as Joe and Noisy. They walked across the sand and Carney Lee's eyes flickered to the ground. Then his brow furrowed in a scowl and he looked even harder.

Halting by the body, Joe, slightly the taller of the two cowhands, scratched his stubby jaw, spat and growled, "That greaser's got him at last."

"How?" asked the Kid mildly.

"How?" snorted Noisy, a gangling, bearded man who rarely said much at all. His eyes went to the sign, then bugged out as they read the message of the marks in the sand. "Hell yes! How?"

"Throwed it in!" suggested Joe, also reading the sign and drawing the too-obvious conclusion.

"Throwed it in . . . all of fifty yards?" said the Kid, indicating the sign. "That'd be some throw. I don't reckon even ole Jim Bowie himself could have made it.''

"You boys likely heard of the Ysabel Kid," Carney Lee remarked casually as Joe opened his mouth to growl some reply.

The change in the two men was instant. The suspicion left them and they both grinned amiably. The Kid was well known. He was regarded by them as a wild young heller who would not hesitate to bend the law if he thought there was need for such action. He was also known as a reader of sign who had few if any peers and as a man who could handle and throw his knife as well as the old Texas master, James Bowie.

"Noisy," growled Carney Lee. "You head for Tasselton. Watch how you cross the ford here, don't mess up the sign. And watch how you pass the Kid's hoss, happen you don't want a leg chewed off. Joe, you go back to the herd and bring young Hughie Hurley back with you. I'll stay on here with the Kid and wait for you to get back."

The men obeyed without question. Noisy brought his horse across the sand, keeping clear of the sign and avoiding the Kid's big white stallion which watched him with malevolent eyes. The other man went to his horse, mounted and headed back in the direction they'd come.

Returning to his horse, the Kid loosed the girths and removed the bridle. Carney Lee joined him after attending to his own, then rolled a smoke and offered one to the Kid.

"Ole Devil sent you along?"

"Soon as he heard from the Judge. Looks like I came too late. You'd best tell me what it's all about. I reckon your hand meant Don Miguel when he said the greaser. Him and the Judge still feuding?"

"As ever they was. That's not what the Judge wanted you along for. Mig wouldn't steal nothing and the Judge knowed it," Lee replied. "Judge wanted you along to try and help us get whoever it is that's rustling our stock and tried to kill him."

"That's what the letter said," agreed the Kid. "How come you boys were out this way?"

"We're working a herd, branding and earmarking some of them for shipment. Saw the Judge's horse coming and took to looking."

That was to be expected. A man afoot on the range was in bad trouble and a riderless horse was always cause for concern. The hands would come out looking for him as soon as they saw their boss's horse. The Kid found nothing unusual in Lee's reply; it was as he'd expected. But there was a lot he wanted to know about the conditions prevailing on this stretch of range. All he knew at the moment was that he'd received an order from Ole Devil Hardin to come to Tasselton County and lend Judge Hurley a hand with some rustler trouble. Now it appeared there was more than just rustler trouble involved.

"You'd best tell me about it, Carney," he suggested.

"Ain't much to tell," replied the other man. "It happened on us all of a sudden at the end of the spring roundup. We'd lost nearly three thousand head over the last year."

The Kid gave a low whistle. That was rustling on a grand scale; three thousand head of cattle would take a fair amount of handling. To take so many in a bunch would need at least eighteen men. A full scale roundup would be necessary to gather them in. Even on the vast open ranges of Texas such a thing could not be done in secret.

"Must have been a steady going on for some time," remarked the Kid. "How about your crew, they all saints?"

"The regular boys are," Carney answered; a saint meant a cowhand who would not work in with the rustlers. "But you know how it is, a man can't keep a full crew these days, has to use regulars in the trail drives and take on what he can. I'd trust Noisy, Joe and maybe three of the others and the rest never gave me no call not to trust them.''

"Don Miguel been losing much?''

"Not according to Alarez. I went over to hold a foreman's jawing session with him a couple of days back. Alarez allows they turned up a couple of our steers which'd been hairbranded.''

"Which same means that some of your roundup crew were working in with the rustlers,'' the Kid pointed out. "The branders'd have to be, and your tally man might have something to do with it.''

"Brander might. I was using Noisy and a new man, real good man with an iron. Not the tally man. It was Judge Hurley's nephew.''

"I never knew he had one,'' the Kid remarked. He knew that it was possible for a man who was really skilled to hairbrand a steer while the roundup was in progress. Burning the brand on the animal's hair without touching the hide, so that when the hair grew out the brand would go with it. It would be no use doing so unless the tally man, recording the amount of cattle handled, worked with him.

"How long's this nephew been with the Judge?''

"Come out just afore the roundup. You know the Judge warn't much of a hand at paper work. Had him that young dude, Jeff Dawson, to handle that sort of work for him most of the time. Then he heard from the nephew, a sister the Judge'd near on forgot about's son. Was satisfied the boy really was kin and, having none of his own, sent for the boy to come,'' replied Lee, knowing the Kid needed to know the local set up. "Jeff didn't cotton none to the idea, not when the Judge told him that young Hughie, him being the nephew, would be taking over the book wrangling. Judge was fair enough about it, told Jeff he could stay on as a hand at the same pay as he was pulling down as bookkeeper.''

"It'd have been this Dawson who'd be tally man,

happen the Judge's nephew hadn't come out," re-marked the Kid thoughtfully. "How about the Judge saying there was a try at killing him?"

"Sure, was at that. Somebody took a shot at him as he was working in his office. Must have come through the window, the bullet. He was in the room on his own. Would have been killed but he dropped something and bent to pick it up just as the shot came. We made us a search all round, but couldn't find nothing. I checked all the hands' guns but warn't none of them just been fired."

"The bullet come through the window? Bust it?"

"Nope, you know how the Judge liked to have the windows open, allowed the scent of the mesquite helped him think."

"What was the Judge doing?"

"Writing a letter to his nephew, telling him to come on out. When Hughie come he showed he was smart as a whip, for a dude. He'd been learning about bookkeep-ing at this fancy Eastern college and took a tally-taking like the devil takes after a yearling. Only had Jeff help him out for half a day."

"There's been any hard talk about Mig not losing stock?" asked the Kid, his eyes going to the still form on the ground.

"Some, you know what these hotheads are."

"Where'd the Judge been; where was he coming back from?"

"Tasselton. He went in last night; never said a word to any of us about what he was fixing to do."

"Strange looking knife that," the Kid drawled, stub-bing his cigarette butt out. "I never saw one quite like it."

With that he walked across the sand toward the body and Carney Lee followed him. They halted by the body and stood looking at it. The Kid's attention was on the knife hilt. For the first time he noticed it was a dull black color with the end charred as if it had been lying near a fire. Dropping his hand the Kid touched the hilt with his finger, and saw a small black smudge on the tip. Then he studied the angle at which the knife had entered the back, rose and stepped carefully astride the tracks of the Judge's horse and looked back over his shoulder.

"See you in a minute, Carney," he said.

Carney Lee did not reply; he was looking across the range and shaking his head sadly. The death of the rancher hit him badly; they'd been friends for more years than he could remember. The Judge had never been a man of letters. His name came, not from law, but from being a good judge of horses and corn liquor. Now he was dead, murdered, and the old foreman swore he would get the man who had killed him.

The Ysabel Kid turned and walked back across the sand to the woods, looking back at the body as if trying to get his bearings. Then he went through the trees his eyes on the ground. He turned and looked back, the body and the sand patch was hidden by trees and bushes. A few steps further on he found what he was looking for. A tree had fallen and there was a clear view of the Judge's body. There was sign on the ground, sign which was plain to the Kid, even though half removed. The Kid lay on the ground behind the tree and looked over. He could see one small patch through the gaps in the trees, a clear opening of about two feet, with no branches or anything in the way.

"About sixty yards, I'd say," he remarked. "That'd take some practice."

With the words he turned and began to track the sign. The man had known what he was doing; he covered his tracks well and might have deceived a less-skilled trailer than the Kid. Even the Kid did not find it easy to follow the man to where he'd left his horse. There were droppings to show the horse had stood for some time, at least half an hour.

"No point in trailing him now," the Kid said to himself, a habit he had picked up on the long, lonely scouts he often took when riding herd or in time of trouble.

Turning, he walked back to the edge of the woods and found Carney Lee waiting for him. The foreman was clearly curious and could not restrain his curiosity any longer.

"What you been doing?" he asked.

"Now that ain't a gentlemanly question," replied the Kid with a grin. "I'd've brought you a piece back on a leaf if I'd known."

"Took you long enough to do *that*," grunted Lee sardonically. "You wants to try taking croton oil."

"Who gets the spread now the Judge's dead?" the Kid asked, disregarding the foreman's cold eyes.

"Hughie, I reckon."

"He with the herd you were working?"

"Nope, stayed on at the spread; said he'd meet us out there but he hadn't showed when I left to look for the Judge," Lee answered, and there was suspicion in his eyes. "You find something in there?"

"Might be something, might be nothing," answered the Kid. "How far round do you reckon that knife hilt'd be? Bigger'n a .45, or even a .50 barrel?"

"Sure, near on an inch. Twice as big as a .50. You reckon the Judge was shot fust, then the knife shoved in to make it look like that was how he died?"

"Nope, I don't reckon that at all. I'm real interested in knives. Just like the Judge and ole Mig are interested in long guns."

The Kid stopped talking. There was a thoughtful look on his face as he looked at the edge of the trail, then toward the body and finally toward the woods. Things were beginning to tie into a pattern but there was just one small thread missing. One thing he had to tie in to make him sure his theory was correct. Every other thing he saw—the knife hilt, the way the Judge's body lay and the horse tracks—tied in, but there was one little thing missing.

Hooves sounded on the trail behind them; three riders

were coming at a fair speed. It was almost an hour since the foreman had sent off his riders and both were returning at the same time, for, even as Noisy came into view with two more men, Joe and another rider came hurtling toward them from the other side.

The Ysabel Kid studied the two men with Noisy. One wore range clothes; he was a tanned, grey-haired man belting a brace of guns and sporting a sheriff's star on his vest. He looked a hard, but honest lawman; the Kid remembered him from the old days: Sheriff Eb Alberts. He looked at the Kid, recognizing him and nodding a greeting.

The other man was also known to the Kid. Doc Jerkin, lean, bald and amiable, good customer from the Kid's smuggling days.

There was no time for small talk. The sheriff swung down from his horse, keeping it off the sand. He looked at the body, then nodded to the doctor who dismounted and followed him toward the body.

"Keep off the sign, Eb!" said the Kid and the urgent note in his voice made the sheriff look down at the horse tracks, then step clear of them.

The doctor bent over the body, glanced at the knife, then knelt and took a closer look. He straightened up and shrugged. "Can't do a thing here. If I can, I'd like to take the Judge over to his place."

The other two riders came up, Joe and a good-looking young man. His clothes were those of a working cowhand but his Stetson did not sit at the correct "jack-deuce angle over his off-eye." It showed him as a dude, a newcomer to the cattle country for such men rarely managed to wear a Stetson in the cowhand manner. His face was pallid under the sun-reddening; he was obviously badly shaken, or so it appeared.

He came across the sand fast, halting by the body and swaying. The sheriff shot out a hand to support the young man, gripping his right shoulder and bringing a wince of pain.

"Shoulder hurt?" asked the Kid mildly.

"A little," the young man replied, his tones not Western. "I bruised it using a Buffalo Sharps."

"Telled you it'd be too much for you," grunted Lee. "You would listen to Jeff Dawson. You don't need a .50 Sharps for shooting mule deer."

The young man stood staring at the body. Joe was still waiting; he'd a horse fastened to his saddle horn to take the body back to the ranch. None of the men spoke for a moment, then the young dude asked:

"Who did it?"

"We don't know yet," answered the sheriff. "Were you with the herd, Hughie?"

"No. I got lost on my way out to them. I only just found them," Hughie Hurley replied. "And I thought I was getting to know my way round the range. That's a knife in Uncle Sam's back."

"Sure," agreed the sheriff.

"Then you'd better arrest the Mexican. The man who owns the next ranch."

"Why?" asked the Kid.

"Everybody knows he and my uncle weren't friends."

"We'll go and tell Mig, anyways," said the sheriff. "You'd best come, Hughie. And you too, Carney, Lon. The boys can help Doc take the Judge back to the spread."

"Jeff Dawson told me there was bad blood between my uncle and that Mexican!" Hughie raised his voice. "Are you going to make an arrest?"

"Sure I am," the sheriff replied. "Just as soon as I find out who done it."

The men loaded the body across a saddle, covering it with a trap. Then Carney Lee gave orders to the two cowhands.

"Don't you pair start talking about how the Judge was killed, or anything," he snapped. "We don't want some fool yelling for war with the Mexicans over it."

"We know ole Mig wouldn't do nothing like this," Joe answered. "We won't say nothing at all."

"I'll see they don't," grunted the doctor.

The rest of the men, the sheriff, Lee, Hurley and the Kid got their horses and rode across the range. Dropping to Alberts's side, the Kid remarked, "That sign back there read a mite strange, Eb."

"What's strange about it?" grunted Alberts. "The Judge rode out there easy enough. He allus come back from that ways and—"

Alberts stopped speaking. His eyes had unconsciously studied the sign as he went to the body, but it had only just struck him how strange it was. His eyes went to the Kid, trying to read something in the Indian-dark, almost babyishly innocent face. He failed and wondered how much the dark youngster knew, how much the sign told him. There was no chance to ask, for Lee and Hurley caught up with them.

"Any idea where the Judge went in town, Carney?" asked the Kid.

"Nope, he usually tells me; didn't this time."

"He went into the telegraph office," the sheriff remarked. "Funny, I saw him coming out of it just afore sundown last night. He stopped at the hotel overnight and never came down to the Lone Star for a drink or a game of poker. Was aiming to ask him about it but he come stomping out of the telegraph office and on to his hoss without giving me a chance."

The Kid lounged in his saddle, thinking fast. The pieces were beginning to fall into place, yet there was something vital missing. He wondered who the Judge was telegraphing. It could not be Ole Devil for Judge Hurley knew a man would be riding as soon as Ole Devil received the letter but could not possibly reach Tasselton County earlier than this morning. The Kid wished Dusty, Mark or even young Waco was here to help him. There were things he wanted to talk over and nobody here he could trust.

They rode up to a big, old Spanish-style building, white walled and cool. Several *vaqueros* were standing around the corral, looking at the approaching party with interest but not animosity.

Don Miguel Hernandez came from the front door of his home as the riders drew rein outside. He was a tall, slender man, grey haired, at least fifty years old but still ramrod straight. He was one of the finest type of Mexican *hildalgo*, brave, a shrewd businessman and a gentleman in the strictest sense of the word. He strode forward to meet the guests, a smile of welcome on his face.

"*Saludos*, Eb, Carney, Mr. Hurley," he said, then his eyes went to the Ysabel Kid and the smile grew even more warm. "*Cabrito*, it has been long since I last saw you. You will stay the night, all of you?"

"Ain't just a-visiting Mig," replied the sheriff. "We found Judge Hurley this morning."

"How did the old goat get himself lost?" Hernandez answered, smiling. "I always said he didn't know this country and—"

"We found him dead, at the Dry River ford."

The Ysabel Kid was watching Hernandez as the sheriff replied. There was no doubt that the Mexican was genuinely shocked at the news. His face showed it for a brief instant, then he got control and relapsed into the expressionless mask which gave nothing away.

"Got a knife in his back," the Kid said gently.

Hernandez wiped a hand across his face, shook his head as if to clear it and gave a sigh. "Poor old Sam," he said. "We had our little quarrels—"

"This wasn't a little one," Hurley put in, his voice throbbing with grief and anger. "Everybody knows you and my uncle were enemies. You could have been waiting for Uncle Sam at the ford and—"

"And what?" asked the Kid, before any of the others could say a word.

"Everybody knows Mexicans use knives," Hurley

finished lamely, for he was a dude and did not know how to read sign. He had not read the strange message in the sand.

"So do other folks," replied the Kid. "This ain't a running iron I've got on my belt."

For all the Kid's words there was tension in the air. The *vaqueros* were gathered around and muttered angrily at the insult to their master. Carney Lee dropped his hand to his side. He did not agree with what the young man had said, but Hughie Hurley was the Judge's nephew and Lee's boss, so the old ranch foreman was ready to defend the youngster from the consequences of his rash words. It was an explosive situation and one which needed delicate handling.

The Kid's words relieved some of the tension and Hernandez spoke gently, showing no offense at the insult.

"Come inside, all of you. The boy is disturbed by his uncle's death and he means nothing by the words."

"Sure," Lee replied. "You'd best know one thing, Hughie. Your uncle and Don Miguel here've been feuding for the pasty thirty years, but they've never stopped being friends. Remember that time Mig bought some fancy rifle that the Judge wanted, Eb?"

"I'll never forget it," answered the sheriff, grinning. "Judge come to town breathing fire and smoke. Told Mig that he was going to start shooting the next time they met. Wanted to step into the street and settle it like gentlemen. You'd have thought there'd be killing certain sure. Then word come that a bunch of Santanta's Kiowa bucks were raiding Mig's herd. Damned if Mig and the Judge didn't get their hosses and ride out side by side to handle them Kiowas."

"Was another time," Lee went on, looking hard at young Hurley. "The Judge bought one of the Volcanic rifles out from under Mig's nose. They wasn't talking for a month after that. Mig come off a hoss, got hurt bad. Your uncle went East to fetch back a doctor who knowed more'n Doc Jerkin about bone setting. Brought Mig a Volcanic rifle back, help get him over his fall.''

The Kid nodded in agreement. The feud between Judge Hurley and Miguel Hernandez was due to their hobby of collecting firearms. It was never so serious that it could not be put off when there was trouble and cooperative action was needed.

Hurley looked embarrassed, but held out his hand. ''I'm sorry, sir. I was misled by what the hands at the ranch told me. My uncle was most uncomplimentary about you, and I heard that you and he were enemies.''

''Come in and I'll show you the latest cause for our enmity.''

The men went into the house, following Don Miguel to the large room used as library and study. For a moment the Kid thought he was back at the OD Connected, except that Ole Devil Hardin's interest was handguns and the Mexican collected rifles. With the eager air of a collector showing off his prizes. Hernandez waved the others to chairs and called to a servant to bring refreshments for his guests.

The walls of the study were covered with long arms of almost every kind and variety. There were muskets of the snapchance, wheel lock-, flintlock- and percussion-fired mechanisms. Single-, double-, quadruple-barreled long arms and early experimental repeating muzzle loaders. The Kid looked at the weapons for he was a rifle shot beyond peer and a keen student of long arms. He recognized an old Ferguson rifle, the earliest attempt at making a breech loading weapon, at least the earliest successful attempt. There were cartridge rifles of many kinds; a line of Winchesters, starting with the forefather of the family, the Volcanic rifle, the Henry and a couple of types of the old yellow boy, the Model of '66. A rifle of the newer Model 73 pattern was underneath, but below that was a gun which made the Kid catch his breath. It was this gun Don Miguel picked up, brought to them and held out with the joy of a collector.

The rifle was a Model 73, a weapon the Kid had seen but not managed to obtain. A Model 73 as he only dreamed about. The woodwork was black walnut, finely carved and checked. The metal was deep blued, finely engraved, and on the top of the barrel was printed the words, "One of a Thousand."

"This is the latest bone of contention," Hernandez said, showing the rifle with some pride. "The Winchester Company are selecting their finest barrels and making up these special rifles. I managed to get the only one the Company held and old Sam was furious. He's got to wait—"

The words died as he realized Judge Hurley would never have one of the magnificent "One of a Thousand" rifles now.

The Kid was looking at it with the expression of a man seeing visions. He'd admired the Model 73, but this was beyond anything he'd ever seen and he knew that one way or another, he must get one. It was at that moment that the Kid saw something which took his attention off the Winchester. He came to his feet and walked across the room to a weapon which hung in the place of honor over the fireplace.

It was all of seven-foot long and appeared to be at least an inch across the muzzle. It was an old-fashioned musket, a flintlock, as the hammer and frizzen pan showed.

Looking up at the gun, the Kid remarked, "I never saw one this size. I'd bet it'd kick like a Missouri mule. A man'd need muscles on his muscles to lift and fire it."

Hernandez knew the Kid was interested in long arms and came forward with the pride of a collector showing off his favorite piece. "He wouldn't hold it and fire from the shoulder. It's a wall gun and meant to be fired from a rest. Originally it would have been rested on the wall of a fort to fire at an attacker. You are right when you say you've never seen one this size before. There are very few of them and this is the longest. A London,

England, gunsmith called John Thomson made it in the late 1600's and it is still in working condition. I've often meant to try it out but my bones are too brittle for the kick." He paused and sighed. "This was another cause of our feud. Sam bought a wall gun, but it was a foot shorter; he never forgave me for that."

"That's a real fancy piece all right," the Kid drawled.

Hernandez turned back to the other men. "Excuse me, please, I get carried away when I talk of my collection. You say Sam was killed by a knife?"

The Kid reached up and ran a finger around the inside wall of the gun's barrel then looked at it. He turned and joined the others who were drinking coffee brought in by a barefoot peon.

"Like you to come on over to the Judge's house for the inquest, Mig," the sheriff said.

"Of course," the Mexican answered. "We'll ride as soon as you've finished your coffee."

Judge Hurley's ranch was much the same in appearance as the Hernandez place. The ranch crew were sitting around, outside the bunkhouse, silent, with none of the usual rowdy horseplay. Doc Jerkin came to the door of the ranch and watched the sheriff and the others leave their horses in the stable at the right of the house.

"I brought the Judge in. Undertaker's come and laid him out ready for the burying. I reckon he'd want to be buried on the place, Hughie. We'll talk about it later on. I left the body in the library, locked the door."

They heard the sound of a horse and turned to see who was coming. One of Alberts' deputies came racing up to a sliding halt. He'd ridden hard and his face showed there was something badly wrong.

"Eh," he gasped, swinging down from his horse. "Ole Joe Tucker's been killed. We found him dead in the post office, shot through the head."

The Ysabel Kid turned to the doctor. "Did you go through the Judge's pockets when you brought him in, Doc?"

"Nope, left it for the sheriff, why?"

Ignoring the sheriff who was talking with the deputy, the Kid went to the door of the house. "Let's take a look at them right now."

The doctor led the way into the hall, his hat and bag were on a small table along with a sheet of paper and a pencil. The Kid glanced at the paper in passing, it was half covered with writing and there was a black smudge on the top of it.

Taking a key from his pocket the doctor opened the door that led into the library. The Kid went in first, his gun in his hand. The room was dark and still. At one end of it a large table showed through the darkness; on it was a bulky, sheet-covered shape.

The doctor brought a lamp from one of the other rooms. His eyes went to a chair and the coat which lay by its side. "That's strange, I hung the Judge's coat over the chair," he said.

The Kid went forward, lifting the coat and seeing what he expected. The pockets had been turned out. Turning to the doctor, the Kid said, "You'd best get Eb in here, Doc."

Alberts arrived fast; he came into the room followed by Hughie Hurley and Carney Lee. They looked around; the young man went to the office desk, bending down to look at the door.

"Somebody tried to break in here," he said.

The others went to the desk; there were three deep grooves cut into the wood around the lock as if someone had been trying to find some way to open it. The sheriff gave an angry growl, turned and went to the windows, trying each one of them in turn. He looked puzzled as he turned back to the others.

"Who came in here, Doc?" he asked.

"Only me and the undertaker, after the boys helped to get the Judge in. Then when we was finished I came out and locked the door."

"Then how the hell did anybody get in?" growled

Alberts indicating the windows. "These're both fastened on this side."

The Kid crossed the room fast, looking at the windows; they were both securely fastened and so was the door. He looked around the big study; the walls were lined with rifles. It was a plainly furnished room, a big table, an assortment of chairs, a well filled bookcase and the desk. There was nowhere a man could be hiding; yet someone had come in and left again.

Carney Lee strode to the table where the body lay, bending to look under it. He straightened up again. "Didn't come through the trapdoor, the bolts are still shot."

Crossing the room the Kid bent over, looking at the trapdoor. The bolts were shot across and were rusted as if the trapdoor was not used. It was quite likely for the door led to a small cellar where the family could hide in case of attack. Now it was connected with the other cellars of the building.

"Who all's got keys to the room here?" asked the Kid.

"I have," Hughie replied. "I think Jeff Dawson had one and my uncle."

"Wouldn't have done anybody any good to have a key," growled the doctor. "I been outside that door, writing my report, ever since the undertaker finished laying the Judge out. There ain't been nobody in or out of it."

"Where's this Dawson gent now?" asked the Kid.

"Went hunting last night," Hughie replied. "He came and asked me where the Judge was, then said he was going on a hunting trip when I told him Uncle Sam'd gone to town. He often went when there wasn't much work on so I didn't object. Besides, it'd give me a chance to work on the books. Jeff uses a system I've never seen before but I think I'm getting the hang of it now."

"Did the undertaker empty the Judge's pockets?" asked the Kid.

"Nope. We allus leave that sort of thing to the sheriff," answered the doctor. "I can't see how the hell anybody could get in and out of here with all the doors locked."

"We could make a search of the cellars," Alberts suggested. "Although I don't see how the hell a man could get down there. The trapdoor's bolted from the top. I don't even think the bolts'd work."

"I've heard these places sometimes have secret passages," Hughie remarked, eyeing the walls with interest.

"Not this'n," Carney Lee answered. "I was here when it was built, there ain't no secret passages in it."

"Look," said the Kid. "We're all tired now, we've had us a long day. Why'n't we get us some sleep and get together in the morning?"

"I can't make it until noon at the earliest," Alberts replied. "I've got to ride back to town and look into the other killing."

"We'll hold us a hearing at one o'clock tomorrow then," suggested the doctor. "See if we can't work something out."

"What's in the desk?" asked the Kid as they turned to leave the room.

"Uncle Sam's cash box; there's usually a fair bit of money in it. He usually keeps a bottle of best bonded whisky in it."

"That all?"

"All the books and paperwork of the ranch are in there, too."

The Kid looked thoughtfully around. "That's a tolerable pile of books I'd reckon," he mused.

"Not too many," Hughie answered.

"Reckon I'll turn in," said the Kid. "You reckon you'd best keep one of the hands out in the hall, and leave the lamp burning here, Carney?''

"Might be as well," Lee replied, knowing the Kid would never make such a request without good reason. "I'll get Joe, Noisy and one of the other old hands to spell each other."

The men were at the door when the Kid turned, looking back at the weapons which hung on the walls and particularly at a fine Remington Rolling Block rifle which hung over the center of the fireplace. He stood looking at it for a moment, then turned and left the room.

The following morning the men gathered outside the room where they ate their meals. The Ysabel Kid was talking with Carney Lee and the ranch foreman nodded his agreement. Then they trooped into the room and sat at the table. The meal was almost silent. Just before they finished, Carney Lee turned to Hughie Hurley and said:

"What do you want the hands to do today, boss?"

"Put them to whatever you think needs doing, Carney." Hughie replied, making the answer he'd heard his uncle give each day since his arrival.

"Are you going to work on the books, Hughie?" asked the Kid. "It might be best to have them all ready for when the Judge's lawyer comes out."

"You're right, Lon," Hughie agreed. "It'll take me all day to do it. I wish Jeff Dawson was here. Do any of you boys know where he might be?"

"Never telled us, Hughie," replied one of the men. "He don't have much truck with us common folks."

The Kid rose, stretched and announced he was going to ride the bedsprings out of his horse. The other men were to be working around the spread, or riding the nearer ranges so as to be on hand for the funeral which was due to start in a couple of hours.

Before the Kid got his horse he saw several men riding out to begin work. He caught his big white, saddled it and swung up. The horse snorted but the Kid rode out without fuss. Then the white settled down to serious work, carrying the Kid across the range.

Once clear of the ranch house the Kid halted and took his bearings. It was some time since he'd ridden this range and then only on odd visits, with a load of contraband. However, his senses worked well; once he saw a range he never really forgot it. He knew what he was looking for and also roughly where to find it. So when he started his horse he was making for a definite place.

He went through three large *bosques*, examining the trees and looking around for final proof of the theory he had formed.

In the fourth *bosque* he found something. Swinging down from his saddle he looked at the sign on the ground, then advanced along the tracks. He went slowly, every sense working for he knew he was dealing with a dangerous enemy, a man who would not hesitate to kill. In the center of the *bosque* was a tree sloped valley with a fairly open bottom. The Kid left his horse at the top of the slope and went down on foot. A tree trunk lay across the bottom of the valley and further along were several more growing. Glancing at the trunk of the fallen tree the Kid studied certain marks around it, then walked to the nearest of the growing trees, also examining the trunk. Nodding in satisfaction the Kid went to the next tree; he moved along the line, glancing back to check on the distance. Stopping by one tree he bent forward and drew out his bowie knife, digging into the wood to extract something.

The big white horse snorted loudly from the top of the slopes. Instantly the Kid's ears detected a faint noise on the other side. A shot rang out and the Kid spun round, falling out of sight behind the tree, his old Dragoon gun in his hand. He lay without a move, out of sight of the man who had shot at him from the top of the other slope.

Time ticked by; the Kid lay still, watching his horse and listening. There was a scuffling sound on the other slope, the big white horse turned its head to whatever was moving. By watching his horse the Kid knew the man was slipping down the slope, coming toward him, and he prepared to hand out a real surprise.

The footsteps drew near; the Kid tensed and lunged forward, his Dragoon gun slanting up.

"Hold it!" he snapped.

A cowhand the Kid remembered seeing in the dining room at the ranch stood at the foot of the slope, a revolver in his hand. He was fast, very fast. The Colt came up and roared, lashing flame at the Kid but the man was off balance and missed. The Kid felt the wind of the bullet by his cheek and shot back, throwing a .44 round, soft lead ball into the man. The Kid shot to kill: a man as fast as this was way too fast to take chances with. The man rocked on his heels, a hole in the center of his forehead and the back of his head shattered wide open.

Leaping forward the Kid kicked the man's gun to one side, then looked down at him. It was a pity there'd been no other way of handling the matter. The man, alive and talking, would have been more use to him.

Gun in hand the Kid went up the slope fast, like a Comanche Dog Soldier hunting a white scalp. Keeping to every bit of cover he could find, he reached the top. He could see the sign left by the man and followed it, but went with caution. The tracks led him through the woods to a small cave. For a moment the Kid stood outside, then darted forward with his gun out. He flattened by the side of the cave, listening for some sound to warn him that others were about.

For a moment he waited, then flung himself in through the opening, his gun lined. The cave was empty but had been used regularly. In one corner lay a pile of blackened embers; the Kid went to these, touching them and finding they were still warm. The man who'd tried to kill him must have been burning some papers here.

Without relaxing, or holstering his gun, the Kid went

over the cave, studying the sign on the ground. Three men regularly used the cave and had been doing for some time. A hole had been scraped in the ground and a large, flat rock lay by it, dragged aside to allow the papers to be burned, the Kid thought. He turned and left the cave, finding tracks where two men had talked, then separated. One was the man the Kid had killed; the other set went off to where two horses had been tied. Only one horse remained now but there were tracks to show which way the other went. The Kid, glancing at the sun, knew he would have to go back to the ranch for the inquest.

For all his hurry the Kid was cautious, there was still danger. The man he was after, the man who killed Judge Hurley, would not hesitate to kill again.

The burial was over and the inquest convened when the Kid came back. There was little enough to be said. The Judge had been murdered by a knife, killed by person or persons unknown. That was the verdict reached and the Kid did little or nothing to add to or help clear up the mystery. He just stated the plain facts: that he'd been on his way to see the Judge, found him dead and waited until Carney Lee came up. He did not mention the things he saw in the woods and Lee, taking his cue from the Kid, said nothing about it either.

The library and office was cleared; only the Kid, the sheriff, Lee, Hughie, and the doctor remained. They waited while the cowhands left the room then Carney Lee looked at the Kid.

"You was some close mouthed just now, Lon."

"Pays to be," replied the Kid.

"Not when there's been two killings—" growled the sheriff.

"Three!"

The sheriff stopped speaking at the Kid's quiet interruption. All eyes went to the dark young man. For a moment none of them said a word, then Alberts snapped, "Who was the other?"

"One of the Judge's hands. Tried to kill me in a *bosque* about four-mile from the spread. Tall jasper, dark, looked about thirty or so. Wore a staghorn handled Colt gun, looked like a tophand."

"McMurry!" Lee spat the word out. "You allow he tried to kill you?"

"Took a couple of shots at me," replied the Kid. "I had to kill him; he was too fast for me to handle any other way."

"Why'd he want to kill you?" the sheriff put in grimly.

"I've made a tolerable few enemies in my short and sinful life. That could have been why – or because I was looking at something I shouldn't have been."

"Such as?" Alberts asked.

"Pieces chipped out of some tree trunks."

From the way the Kid spoke, Alberts knew there was no point in continuing the questioning. He wanted to get at the mystery, but knew that once the Kid dug in his toes there was no shifting him. If the worst came to the worst, the Kid would forget how to speak English and go over to pure Comanche, which Alberts did not speak.

"This here McMurry," said the Kid. "He worked these parts for long?"

"Took on for the roundup." Tophand, good with cattle but a mite close mouthed. He was one of the best hands I ever saw with a branding iron."

"He was one of your branders on the last gather?"

"Sure."

The Kid looked thoughtful. Things were falling into place, dropping in to fit the pattern. He did not mention his ideas yet, but went to where the knife lay on the table. It had been shown in evidence at the inquest but· so far the Kid had not been given a chance to examine it. He took it up, turning it in his hands. The knife was usual in form, looking like a butcher's steel sharpened down to a point. He gave little attention to the blackened hilt, his eyes were on the blade.

The Kid knew knives. His mother had been the daughter of Chief Long Walker and his French-Creole squaw. From both the Kid inherited the knife-savvy of a nation of knife-fighters who knew few, if any, betters. All his life he'd handled knives of various kinds and there was much he knew about them. This knife was all wrong as a fighting weapon, there was no guard to protect the hand from a slash, there was no edge to rip into the knife-fighter's target, the belly. It was a weapon designed purely for murder, for there was only one way it could be used: in a thrust which would sink the point home.

Carefully the Kid tested the balance of the weapon, then gripped it by the point. His hand whipped back and the knife hurled across the room into the wooden shield just below the Remington Rolling Block rifle. The Kid went forward and leaped to catch the rife as the jolt brought it sliding from the pegs.

He rested the rifle back again, seeing that the pegs were set so that the long barrel tip just rested. He turned and looked at the others who were staring at him with undivided attention.

"Sorry," he said. "I was wondering if this knife would throw."

"Looks like it will," Carney answered grimly. He did not know what the Kid was up to, but was willing to go along with him.

"Is that how my uncle was killed, by a thrown knife?"

"Nope."

"You saw the sign, Lon. You're not trying to tell me it was pushed in by hand, are you?" growled Lee.

The sheriff snorted angrily. He could read sign and knew that there was no way this knife could have been pushed in to the Judge's back by hand. The Judge would not, could not, have ridden fifty yards with the knife in his back and there was no sign that another man

was out on the sand. The man could not have been
riding behind the Judge, holding him after killing him,
then pushing him off. The horse tracks proved that;
they were just deep enough to have been made by the
animal carrying the Judge's weight so far, then the right
depth for a riderless horse.

"How the hell did it happen, Lon?" he asked.

"You wouldn't believe me, even if I told you, which
same I won't," answered the Kid. "Like to talk with
Hughie and Carney alone, Eb."

"You will if you want to," replied the sheriff wryly.
"I want to get this lot cleaned up, Lon. Election's due
real soon and I don't want a thing like this hanging over
me."

"Happen we can help you a mite, give us time,"
drawled the Kid and Alberts had faith in his quiet
words.

Alone in the room with Lee and Hughie, the Kid
dropped his voice and told them what he knew, and
what he suspected but couldn't prove. Hughie gave his
agreement with some of it, the stuff he himself knew to
be possible, and was willing to go along with the Kid's
idea.

"I don't know," Lee objected. "It'll be dangerous
and Hughie ain't used to handling anything like this."

"Thing being Hughie won't be handling it. There
can't be a move made until dark and then I'll be here,
not Hughie."

"I can't have that, Kid," Hughie put in. "You're
risking your life to—"

"Sure, but I know what to expect, you don't," answered the Kid. "There'll be no risk if you do your
part."

It took some doing, but Lee and the Kid finally per-
suaded the young man it would be best if he played the
game their way. So Hughie agreed and a few moments
later Carney went out to ask all the men to keep well

clear of the library as Hughie was trying to work out the ranch books and wanted quiet.

"Reckon it'll take him long, Carney?" asked one of the hands.

"Most all day, he reckons. Looks like Jeff made his own system and he's away hunting."

The hands went about their business and Carney slouched off on his own. He joined the Kid in the house some time later. "One of them slipped off," he said. "I let him go, didn't want to make him suspicious."

"*Bueno*," replied the Kid, then turned as Hughie came up to him. "Man, you surely look elegant; ole Mark Counter'd go green if he saw that jacket."

Hughie's face reddened slightly. The green velvet smoking jacket was a present from a maiden aunt and packed by mistake when he came West. The Kid had wanted Hughie to wear something conspicuous. In addition to green velvet, black lapel and collared smoking jacket, he was wearing a fezlike hat, a present from the same maiden aunt. The Kid scowled, thinking Hughie was jobbing him, then grinned as he saw the real reason. Hughie's hair was considerably lighter in color than the Kid's.

The idea was put into practice immediately. Hughie spent the day alone in the office, working on the books and trying to solve Jeff Dawson's system of bookkeeping. The Kid doubted if there would be any danger during daylight and so headed for town to see the sheriff.

It was dark when he rode back, and the ranch crew were eating their supper. Hughie was with them, his coat and hat coming in for a lot of good-natured chaff. The Kid did not make any attempt to join the other men, but headed for the library and slipped in. Keeping well clear of the windows, the Kid moved around the room, checking everything. He looked under the table at the trapdoor, seeing the bolts were shot home. With his search complete he went to wait behind the door.

Footsteps outside sounded to the Kid, the door opened and he heard Hughie saying, "I'm going through with it even if the Kid isn't back, Carney."

"I tell you it ain't safe," Lee replied and they entered carrying a lamp.

Hughie took the lamp and set it on the desk. It gave him a light where he wanted to work but the rest of the room was in deep shadow. The two men stood for a moment, then Carney Lee growled: "I shouldn't let you go through with it, boy. If the Kid's right—"

"I reckon he is."

The two men swung round, Hughie reaching for the lamp and Lee dropping his hand to his side as he saw the dark, shadowy shape. They recognized the voice. It said much for the young Easterner's presence of mind that he did not lift the lamp and let the light shine on the Kid.

"That you, Lon?" Lee hissed unnecessarily.

"Naw, it's Santa Anna," came back the mocking voice. "You'd best get out of here, Carney. You know what to do?"

"Sure I do. I only hope it goes right."

There came a low chuckle from the Kid, his voice sardonic. Lee guessed the mocking, Indian-hard grin was playing on the Kid's face as he replied: "Happen it don't, remember one thing – I don't like lilies."

Carney Lee chuckled, then went to the door. He opened it and walked out, closing it behind him. At the desk Hughie began working on the books, his pen scratched, he checked figures and might have been alone, for the Kid remained silent and unseen in the deep shadows. They did not speak, for that the Kid had insisted on. He doubted if there was any actual danger to the young man until the ranch crew were all asleep but someone might be watching from outside.

A knock on the door brought the Kid's Dragoon gun into his hand, the door opened and the ranch cook entered, tray in hand, bringing coffee and cookies for Hughie.

"Boys are all turning in," the cook said, setting the tray on the edge of the desk. "You going to be working long?"

"I'm fixing to finish the books tonight, Cookie," Hughie replied. "Tell Carney I aim to get them done tonight. Thanks for the coffee."

The cook left without even knowing there was a second man in the room. The Kid holstered his gun and moved silently to the window. He waited until he saw the bunkhouse lights going out one after another, then knew it was time for him to take Hughie's place.

Hughie worked for a few minutes, then rose, stretched and started to pace the room as if working the stiffness out of his bones. He passed in and out of the circle of light three or four times, then stopped in the darkness and quickly removed coat and hat, handing them to the Kid, who slipped them on. The Kid made sure he could move comfortably, then went and sat at the desk, pretending to be working on the books. Hughie sat down in a comfortable chair in the darkness and watched the Kid.

The time dragged by. The Kid was like an Indian in his patience. He tried to carry on as he'd watched Hughie doing, though he doubted if there was any need for such deception. Hughie tried to stay awake in his excitement but after a couple of hours his head began to sag on his chest. He shook it off twice, then went to sleep sitting in the chair.

The Kid pretended to work on. From the steady breathing he knew Hughie was asleep and that was what he wanted. The Kid knew the danger he was in and the risk he was taking; but he also knew his own capability at handling such a situation.

A faint sound came to the Kid's ears; he tensed, ears straining. It was not Hughie moving in his sleep, or his breathing, for the Kid's ears had grown used to both sounds and this one broke through them. It was only a faint noise. The room lay still and dark except for the light which shone on the Kid as he sat at the desk.

There was a faint hissing sound; the Kid heard and moved with all the speed he could manage. Throwing himself from the chair, he lit down on the floor, rolling back into the darkness. There was a roar, and a spurt of flame from under the table. Something hissed through the air, and thudded into the desk. The Kid hit the floor with his Dragoon gun in his hand. He was blinded by the muzzle flash from under the table, but he shot back by instinct. He heard a thud, as if something wooden fell to the floor, then he was on his feet and hurling toward the door. Hughie was awake; his senses were muddled for an instant, but he got control of them. As the Kid opened the door, Hughie was grabbing the lamp from the desk. He stopped, staring at the thing which stood quivering in the wood of the desk. It was the hilt of a knife like the one which had killed his uncle.

"Come on, Hughie!" roared the Kid, racing for the front door of the house and jerking it open.

Hughie followed. He heard the Kid running along the side of the house and came out. The Kid turned the corner of the house and shouted a challenge. There was a fast exchange of shots, then a man yelled:

"Don't shoot. I'm hit!"

Turning the corner Hughie saw the Kid advancing on a man who stood at the outside doors of the cellars. The light of the lamp showed the man on his knees, holding his arm. He was a cowhand who worked for the ranch and looked scared as well as in pain. The .44 ball had only grazed his arm but the bicep was ripped wide open.

Light showed from the bunkhouse and Carney Lee appeared carrying a lamp. He was fully dressed and his gun was in his hand. Stopping, he looked at the cowhand and growled, "McMurry's bunkie. Was it him? I heard a shot. Was that—"

"I didn't do it!" yelled the cowhand. "I only opened the door and let Jeff Dawson in."

"Dawson?" growled Carney Lee. "Where is he?"

"Still in the cellars."

The Kid jerked up the cellar doors and went down the steps. He went with caution, gun in hand, ready to shoot. Carney Lee followed. They passed through the Judge's supply cellar and opened a door at the end. Apart from the Judge's ample stock there was nothing to be seen, but there was still another door showing in the light. They went toward it, flatting on either side. The Kid moved fast. He kicked the door open and went in with his old Colt Dragoon ready for action. He found his caution unneeded. Carney Lee's lamp showed a stocky youngish man lying on the floor. He was face up, two bullet holes in his head.

"Jeff Dawson," Lee grunted, then poked down at the long wall gun which lay by the man's side. "You mean that was how he done it?"

There were running steps and the sheriff came in followed by a deputy. They'd come from town with the Kid and stayed out on the range waiting for the shooting to start before moving in.

Some time later, the sheriff, Hughie and Lee were in the library examining the knife while the Kid told them how he'd guessed what had happened.

"I knowed there was something wrong from the sign," he said. "The Judge wasn't knifed, there was no sign near enough. Even had there been it couldn't have been done!"

"Why not?" asked Hughie. "You showed the knife could be thrown."

"Why sure," agreed the Kid. "It could be thrown, but not to stick hilt deep in a man. I don't reckon there's a knife made, apart from a bowie like I carry, that can be sunk hilt deep into a man with a throw. It's a matter of balance and weight, or something. So the knife hadn't been pushed in, hadn't been thrown in. The way the Judge's hoss acted was a pointer. It walked out there easy enough, then something spooked it, made it rear and pitched the Judge. That told me something, it

meant the Judge was killed there. It'd take more than a
hoss rearing to throw him off, unless he'd just been hurt
bad. So I took a look in the woods and found where a
man lay up with a rifle or something. Only the Judge
was knifed, not shot. I touched the knife hilt earlier and
got some black on my finger; thought at first the knife'd
been near fire and got scorched. Knowed different then;
it was powder blackening. The doctor got some on his
hands when he pulled the knife out. I could see what
might have happened, only I'd never seen a gun with a
bore big enough to take the knife. It got me at first, then
I saw it, when Don Miguel said a wall gun had to be
fired from a rest. The man got a rest, the only place he
could hide and the Judge wasn't in sight until he got
halfway across the patch. I checked the muzzle of Don
Miguel's gun while we were at his place; it was a mite
rusty inside so it hadn't been fired. That let him out. I
suspected you, Hughie, but when I took my ride I found
where Dawson practiced with his gun. He'd been doing
it for a fair piece, you'd not been here that long."

"I know why Dawson did it," Hughie answered.
"I've made out enough from the books to know that
he'd been robbing my uncle for at least two years."

"And the Judge got to suspecting him, got the Cat-
tlemen's Association on it," the sheriff growled. "He
went to town to see if there was either a letter or a
telegraph message from them. Got it the morning he
was killed. Dawson shot him, then found he couldn't go
to the body without leaving sign, so left it until the body
was brought back to the ranch. Sneaked back in,
through the cellar, up through the trapdoor—"

"But it was bolted on the top side," objected Hughie.

The Kid laughed, going to the table and pulling it
aside. He gripped the ring and pulled, the trapdoor
lifted straight up, the bolts splitting where the floor
joined and still appearing to be closed.

"That was how he did it. He must have fitted this up
while he was working on the books alone," he drawled.

"Dawson knew he might need to get rid of the Judge one day and got things ready. Tried to kill the Judge that way one night and missed. Then when Dawson heard you was coming out, Hughie, he knew he'd got to move fast. You went out to watch the tally work and took over. McMurry was hair-branding some of the herd and Dawson didn't get a chance to tell him to stop. The other hand told us all about it. He's been talking plenty."

"You were sure it was a wall gun?" asked Hughie.

"Don Miguel told us the Judge had one and I couldn't see it anywhere. It should have been hung over the fireplace but Dawson took it. Then knew the empty space'd be noticed and put the Remington up there. Only the Remington wasn't as long as the wall gun and didn't set safe on the pegs. I wouldn't have noticed, until it fell. Then I looked and saw that the pegs were made for a longer rifle. It was just another thing to point to Dawson. He was the only man other than the Judge and Carney who could come in here at any time. He was the only man with enough time on his hands, when the other boys were on the range, to learn how to use that thing with a knife for a charge. That took some learning. I found the trees he'd used for targets and one with a broken knife in it. That was when McMurry tried to drop me. He'd heard me moving and came to look. I trailed him back to the cave they'd been using to meet away from the spread. Kept their records there but it was too late. McMurry killed the post office gent in town, had to stop him telling about the letter and wires the Judge was sending."

"You wouldn't want to take on as my deputy, would you, Lon?" Albert asked.

The Kid laughed. "I'm already hired, Eb. Couldn't change my job. They know too much about me. One thing I do know, if any of those OD Connected fellers hear about me wearing that green jacket I'll come back here and fix somebody's wagon for good."

Carney Lee and Hughie both laughed. They were looking at the tall, lean, Indian-dark young Texan. He didn't look more than sixteen, yet he packed a world of savvy into his young head. They owed him a lot; he'd saved them from what could have developed into a range war with the Mexicans on the next ranch. He'd helped to break a rustling gang which was costing the ranch hard-earned money and he'd found the man who murdered Judge Hurley.

They owed a lot to the grandson of Chief Long Walker of the Comanches, the ex-border smuggler who now rode as part of Ole Devil Hardin's floating outfit, the Ysabel Kid.